Bite my Bengal

A Paranormal Dating Agency Story

Jeannie,
it's never
too late for love.
Roxanne
Witherell

Roxanne Witherell

For the Love of Fire and Ice

Paranormal Dating Agency

Copyright 2018 Roxanne Witherell

Published by MT Worlds Press, Inc.

Winter Springs, FL 32708

http://mtworldspress.com

Cover art by: Glowing Moon Cover Designs

Edited by: Liz Wilks

Formatting by Celtic Formatting

http://mtworldspress.com

Dedication

For the wonderful BJ in my life. Thank you, Barbara June, for all the faith and love you give.

Acknowledgment

I want to send out a special thanks to Milly Taiden for creating the wonderful world of Paranormal Dating Agency. I look forward to writing many more books in the PDA world.

One

"Are you sure it's a good idea for us to go to Heads N' Tails?" BJ asked Braelynn as they rounded the corner of the tall building.

"It'll be fine. Annette's meeting us at the restaurant." Braelynn held open the door for BJ to go in.

"This better be one amazing steak," BJ said, stepping up to the front desk.

"Oh, they're the best," Braelynn commented as she handed the receptionist her membership card. "Hi, Tyra."

"It's good to see you, Braelynn. Sign here." Tyra handed her a clipboard.

Braelynn signed her name and passed the clipboard to BJ. She signed her name beside Braelynn's as a guest, then handed the clipboard back to Tyra. BJ didn't see why they needed to sign in just to go to the restaurant.

Braelynn assured her it was just for security reasons. If something was to happen then they would be able to look back to see who was there. BJ followed Braelynn into the elevator.

"I got to admit. I'm kind of excited to see where you girls have been the last few months," BJ told her.

"In my defense, I have been inviting y'all forever."

"Yeah, I'll pass on your favorite levels," BJ laughed. "I'll stick with our dinner dates."

"Have it your way." Braelynn shrugged.

The elevator doors opened when they arrived on level eighteen. Soft music played inside the restaurant seeping out into the hallway. Large French doors opened up into a large restaurant. They stopped at the hostess podium. A tall blonde smiled as they approached.

"Welcome to Heads N' Tails," she greeted them. "How many?"

"We're joining Annette tonight," Braelynn told her.

"She just finished her shift." She waved them through. "Right this way."

The hostess led them through the restaurant. BJ noticed Annette sitting at a table near the rooftop doors. They had a clear view of the beautiful star-filled sky. White cloth linens covered the table tops. Each table was lit up with candles. BJ could easily see this as being one of the most romantic restaurants in the city. Too bad it catered mainly to shifters and other paranormals. BJ wouldn't even be there if it wasn't for the fact of Annette falling in love with the owners of Heads N' Tails. Annette started working at the restaurant so Tony and Brian could open more levels of the club and move employees around to cover those floors.

"Annette, this place is gorgeous." BJ gave Annette a hug then sat in the seat next to her. Braelynn sat on the opposite side of Annette.

"Isn't it? Things seem to run smoother here than at Pierre's. I'm glad I made the change," Annette admitted.

The waitress came by with their drinks. Annette must have ordered for them before they arrived. Glancing at the tall glass of what BJ assumed was a Fuzzy Navel, she noticed an extra setting at the table. Usually the hostess would grab the extra setting when all the members of the party arrived.

"Are we expecting someone else?" BJ asked Annette. Braelynn didn't mention anyone joining them.

"Well, we wanted to talk about that." Annette looked down at her watch.

"What did you do?" BJ looked at them.

"I think you should give Paranormal Dating Agency a try," Braelynn said.

"What?" BJ shook her head. "I'm too damn old for that shit. I'm fine just the way I am."

"We know you're fine, but wouldn't you like to be happy?" Annette asked.

"I was happy," BJ told them. Her late husband, Dave, made her happy. "I had my shot. It was great while it lasted. I'm not as young as you two."

"Forty-five isn't old, either," Annette pointed out. "You could find happiness again."

"Plus, she's already on her way." Braelynn grinned.

"No, you didn't." BJ couldn't believe they had this planned out.

"We did," Annette confirmed.

"I can't believe you two would do this behind my back," BJ paused. "You know what? I can believe you two would do this. This is the type of shit that happens when you two get together without supervision. You see this new patch of gray hair right here." BJ pointed out the noticeable gray right at her part line. "This is from you two. You caused this."

"You can barely notice it. Come on, give it a shot. She'll be here in time for dessert," Braelynn said. "Besides, what harm could it do."

BJ sighed and picked up the menu in front of her. She opened the menu even though she already knew what she wanted. Instead, she stared blankly at the menu and thought about Dave. She could never replace Dave, nor would she want to. The moment she met Dave, she knew she wanted to marry him. They started dating when she was 16 and got married a few months after high school graduation. They were only married for 22 years when a motorcycle crash took him from her. That was five years ago, and she still hadn't looked at another. She spent 24 years with the love of her life. You don't get a second chance after that. Dave was the only one for her. She knew that then just like she knew that now. BJ sighed again as she put down the menu. She missed the warmth of Dave's embrace.

"Honey, we didn't mean to upset you." Annette placed her hand on BJ's.

"It's fine," BJ assured her as she fought back the tears that threatened to spill out.

"We just think you could be happy again. Gerri will find you someone that fits you just right," Braelynn told her. "Look what she did for us. Have you ever seen us happier than we are now?"

"No, but you two deserve your happiness," BJ told her.

"You deserve to be happy too," Annette pointed out.

"Let's drop the subject for now," BJ said as the waitress came over to take their orders.

BJ barely spoke at all through dinner. Her steak was cooked to perfection and she practically moaned with every bite. It'd ruined her from going anywhere else for a steak dinner, that was for sure.

"This steak is heaven," BJ commented.

"Told you." Braelynn smiled.

"What else would you expect from a lion shifter? That man knows how to cook meat," Annette told them.

"It still blows my mind, all the different shifters in one place," BJ said.

"I never knew there were so many," Braelynn agreed. "Hell, I didn't know Tony and Bryan were dragon shifters until Ronan told me."

"Most of the time, humans won't know unless they're witches or have a sense for those things," Annette said. "There's a couple I've seen around for years and just found out they're wolves."

"Makes you wonder how many shifters you may actually know," BJ commented.

"Now that I'm with Ronan, shifters seem more open about it around me. They don't hide the fact that they're shifters, but they don't flaunt the fact that they are, either." Braelynn picked up her wine glass and took a sip.

As they finished their meal, the waitress came back with a dessert menu and took their empty plates. BJ looked over the menu; the souffle was practically calling her name. They ordered when the waitress came back around. Annette looked down at her watch for the third time.

"I guess your matchmaker won't make it tonight," BJ stated after the waitress brought their desserts out.

"Guess again." An older woman came up behind Annette. "You must be BJ Elwood. I'm Gerri."

"I remember you from Braelynn's wedding," BJ said shaking Gerri's hand.

"I sense you're not happy to see me." Gerri sat in the chair next to her.

"It's not that I'm not happy to see you. It's just the way these two went about it." She glared at Annette and Braelynn.

"I see," Gerri nodded. "I assure you they have the best of intentions."

"I'm sure they did, but it's not necessary. I'm not looking for a man in my life or in my bed," BJ told her.

"Come on, BJ," Braelynn pleaded. "You'll be glad you did."

"If you were looking for a man, what would you look for?" Gerri asked.

"I'd look for Dave," she said simply. She knew Gerri was just trying to distract her from getting aggravated with her friends, but it didn't matter.

"Okay, then tell me about Dave," Gerri suggested.

"He was the most amazing man I'd ever met," BJ closed her eyes. Dave was a topic she could easily talk about. "His eyes were baby blue. They turned gray when he was sick. His hair was longer than mine and he didn't mind me running my hands through it every chance I got. People would stare at us because of our height difference. Dave was more than a foot taller than me. He was generous to a fault. Never met a person he didn't want to help. He loved working with his hands. Every year he would make me something for my birthday. He would always put me before himself."

"He sounds wonderful," Gerri commented.

"He was." BJ opened her eyes to see everyone at the table staring at her. It was then she realized a tear had fallen down her cheek. She quickly wiped it away. "As you can see, I'm not ready to date again."

"That's only because you haven't met the right person to help you move forward. It's never too late to find another love. If Dave always put you first then you should realize by now that he wouldn't want you to be lonely forever."

Gerri's words rang true. BJ knew Dave would want her to be happy, but all she wanted was Dave. There's no way Gerri could find her someone like Dave. He was one of a kind. BJ sighed and took a bite of her souffle. Thoughts ran through her mind a mile a minute. It did get lonely, especially since all her friends were now married or close enough to it. It would be nice to have companionship.

"I don't think there's anyone out there for me," BJ said sadly. "But if you think you can find another Dave then more power to you."

"You'll do it?" Braelynn questioned with a smile.

"I'll let Gerri try." BJ shrugged. "I doubt much will come of it."

"Oh, don't be so negative." Annette patted her arm. "I swear, Gerri has a magical touch to these things."

"It may take some time to find the right man for you," Gerri told her.

"Now don't go all crazy like you did with Annette," BJ laughed. "I don't need two men. One will be plenty."

"Oh, I had no intention of finding you two," Gerri admitted.

"Good." BJ didn't even need one man, so she damn well didn't need two.

Two

"How much longer do you think it will take?" Bryan asked as he came around the bar.

"On this piece?" Dare carved a sliver of wood away from the side of the bar. "It will be done by Saturday. The columns won't take as long since the detailing isn't small. A couple of weeks and you'll be ready to open. As long as you can keep Tony from coming up with something new."

"Last time he came down with Annette, they added a week's worth of work. I told him they weren't allowed back down here," Bryan said.

"I can't see Tony following that rule." Dare laughed.

"One can only hope." Bryan shrugged. "Tony has enough on his plate shuffling employees around so we can open this level. There's a lot of switching up going around. Some people just can't work with others. Tony will have his hands full for another two weeks."

"We should be able to finish by then." Dare blew on the bar carving, sending wood scrapings flying.

"Excellent." Bryan grabbed the lights off the bar and went back to work.

Dare went back to his carving. The bar carving may go a little faster than he thought. He only had another foot to go on this side. Then all that was left was sanding and staining. The detail had taken longer than expected. Turning the bar into a forest scene hadn't been easy. Once it was all sanded, he'd go back over it with his torch to add depth in some areas.

"We got a lot done today." Bryan finished lining the shelves with LED lights. "I say we call it a night."

"I'm almost to a stopping point." Dare wiped over the freshly sanded carving.

"When you going to take us up on our offer and come have a drink upstairs?" Bryan stepped off the step ladder.

"After Tony hounded me last week, I came prepared." Dare pointed to the duffle bag beside his tool bag. "I just need a place to wash up."

"I can help you with that," Bryan offered.

Dare narrowed his eyes at Bryan, giving him a suspicious look.

"Not like that." Bryan laughed. He pulled his phone from his pocket. "I'll give Tyra a call and she can get you all set up."

"Thanks." Dare went back to his carving while Bryan was on the phone.

In all the weeks that Dare has been working at Heads N' Tails, he hadn't gone to any of the levels other than what was going through renovations. He was contracted to do the woodwork. Once that was done, he'd move on to the next project. He never thought to hang out for a drink. By the time his work was done for the day, he was ready to go home and relax. When he got home, he didn't feel like going out again. He lived to the north of the city, on the edge of the state park. He felt at ease living close to the wooded area.

"You're good to go." Bryan set his phone on the bar top. "Just go to room 413 on the fourth level when you're done here. There will be a beer waiting for you on the ninth level when you're ready."

"I'll wrap things up here and be down in a bit." Dare set down his chisel, picked up his rag and wiped down the area he was working on.

"I'm heading out." Bryan closed up his toolbox. "See you in a little while."

"See ya." Dare wiped down the side of the bar, looking over his work.

Dare started his clean up once Bryan left. Wood shavings littered the floor where he had been sitting. He gathered his tools and dropped them in his tool bag. He swept up the mess on the floor, always leaving the room how he found it. Once everything was back in proper order, he grabbed his overnight bag and headed out.

His membership card now allowed him access to the fourth and ninth floors. Dare had no intention of spending the night in one of the rooms. A quick shower is all he needed to wash away the smell of wood. The elevator ride to the fourth floor only took a minute. He'd make good time, and if he was lucky, he'd be home by midnight.

****

Dare made his way up to the ninth floor. He didn't know what to expect since all the floors were different even though it was part of the same club. As the elevator door slid open, music sounded down the hall. At least he liked the music. He made his way down the hall to the double doors that led into the club. The space was just as large as the one he was working on. Although the layout was different, he was still able to find his way around. There was two serving bars on this level. Dare spotted Tony mixing drinks at the main bar. He made his way over, taking a seat on one of the bar stools.

"I didn't think I'd ever see you down here," Tony gasped dramatically.

"Bryan didn't tell you I was coming?" Dare asked.

"Nah, I haven't talked to him since lunch. Annette's with her friends tonight so Bryan is coming down after he cleans up." Tony looked past Dare and smiled. "Speaking of my love."

"Speaking of me?" Bryan walked up behind Dare, clapping him on the back with a nod. He walked around the end of the bar and kissed Tony's cheek.

"Yeah, I was just saying that you didn't tell me Dare was coming down from the twelfth level to enjoy the living." Tony smacked Bryan's ass as he went by to grab a drink.

"You like surprises." Bryan reached in the cooler and pulled out a beer. He held the bottle out to Dare. "Light, right?"

"That's it," Dare accepted the bottle after Bryan opened it.

Bryan helped Tony as people came up to the bar for drinks. Dare turned in his seat and enjoyed his beer and good music. The only thing that could have made this better was if he was home with a fire going in the pit and a guitar in his hands. Tigers were loners, he couldn't help that he preferred to be alone in the woods rather than surrounded by people. Though it wouldn't hurt to be sociable every once in a while.

A woman came up to the bar. She had to stand on her tiptoes to slide into the high bar stool two spots down from Dare. She glanced over at him and smiled with a nod. Her white hair hung just below her jawbone. Dare nodded in politeness and went back to drinking his beer.

"Gerri, what a pleasure to see you here." Tony leaned over the bar and kissed the woman's cheek.

"I was just upstairs talking with Annette and her friends," she told Tony as Bryan walked up and greeted her. "I thought I would come down here and scope out the place."

"The place or the people?" Bryan asked with a laugh.

"Well, one goes with the other." Gerri shrugged and glanced toward Dare again. "You can tell a lot about people from just watching them in places."

"How's that?" Tony asked.

"Take this guy for example." Gerri nodded in Dare's direction.

He didn't let on that he noticed her movement. Instead, he listened to what she was going to say about him. Ready to correct her when she no doubt got it wrong.

"He's stiff, so he's not really wanting to be here right now. He has a tight grip on his beer. He's probably not a people person. Hard on the outside and probably all warm and soft on the inside."

"Hey, Dare!" Bryan called over to him. "I think she knows you."

"Gerri, I'd like to you meet Dare. He's working with us to get level twelve open. Dare, this is Gerri Wilder. Her goal is to personally see that everyone finds love." Tony smiled as he introduced them.

Dare stuck his hand out to shake Gerri's. She shook his hand then hopped down off her stool. She came over and tiptoed onto the stool next to him. Bryan handed Gerri a martini, and she turned her attention back on Dare. He wasn't sure he was going to like this. Maybe he could dip out shortly.

"What about you?" Gerri asked him. "Have you found love? I can't imagine you having a woman at home if you're all alone here."

"I've loved once, and it didn't end well." He lost Sarah in a fire nearly 20 years ago. Though he would always love her, he had accepted that she was gone forever.

"I'm sorry to hear that." Gerri looked at him with sadness in her eyes. "Like I was telling someone earlier, it's never too late to find another love."

"You think you can find me another love?" Dare laughed. "Shifters have but one true mate."

"In most cases that is right," Gerri agreed. "In some cases though, when a shifter's mate dies and the other survives, there's a chance of another."

"You should let her take a look for you. I'm telling you, Dare. This woman is amazing. She found Annette for us."

Dare thought about it. He hadn't been out in a long time. His days were spent working, and his nights are spent at home relaxing. It wouldn't be too bad to find someone to relax with him. What could it hurt? It's not like he was getting any younger.

"I don't know how you are going to do this with you thinking I don't like people," he joked.

"I said you're not a people person not that you don't like people," Gerri corrected him. "I also said you were warm and soft on the inside. I know it's there."

"Alright, have at it then. I gave up looking for another years ago," Dare admitted.

"That's because you didn't have Gerri," Tony explained.

"I am rather remarkable." Gerri smiled. "I have a knack for it."

"Let's see how good you are then," Dare challenged her.

"Challenge accepted." Gerri grinned. "Here's my card. I'll call you later on with details."

After thirty minutes of casual conversation, Gerri excused herself. There were others in the crowd she wanted to scope out and get to know. Dare gave her a nod and turned his attention to his empty beer bottle. Should he stay or should he go?

"Want another?" Tony asked.

"Yeah, I'll have one more before I get on the road." Dare handed him the empty bottle in exchange for a fresh one.

Why not get used to the idea of having to go out? Maybe Gerri could find him a homebody just like him. Someone who just wants to chill out at home and have a good grilled steak. Someone who enjoys campfires and fishing trips. He didn't want glamorous. A woman all dolled up in tons of makeup and hairspray never got his attention. Sarah had always been badass. Her hair was always pulled back and she didn't mind getting her nails dirty. She would chop firewood and bait her own fishing hook. Dare shook the images from his mind. He loved Sarah dearly, but it was time to find that kind of love again.

Three

BJ stood in her bakery's kitchen, slicing up the cinnamon roll log she had just finished making. They were always a favorite amongst the morning crowd. She still had time before the morning rush came in. A few early birds had already stopped by for their morning coffee and bagels. The bakery had been known for its bagels. Which is why her mother renamed the store, Bite My Bagel, after her grandfather passed away. It brought so much joy to her mother, BJ didn't have the heart to change it.

BJ had just finished arranging the cinnamon rolls on a cookie sheet when the bell above the door rang out. A tall business man stepped through the door carrying a briefcase. BJ slid the cookie sheet into the oven before turning to the new customer.

"Morning, you look like you could use some coffee," BJ greeted him as he stepped up to the counter.

"Ms. Betty Jean Elwood?" he asked.

"Please, just Ms. Elwood is fine." He now had her attention. It's not everyday someone comes calling you by your full name. Her first thought was a lawyer.

"Ms. Elwood," he corrected himself. "Let me introduce myself. I'm Franklin Jones and I work for McNeilsons Incorporated."

"What can I do for you?"

"We recently acquired the connecting properties to your establishment. We're interested in this lot as well," he stated, setting his briefcase down on the counter.

"It's not for sale," she said simply.

"We're prepared to pay more than the appraised value," he countered.

"Mr. Jones, my family has owned this bakery for generations. It's not for sale now nor will it be in the future.

"We don't want the bakery. We only want the building. With the amount you'll get you could easily relocate. He pulled a business card from his briefcase and wrote on the back, then slid it across the counter toward her. "I think you'll find this more than fair."

"I'm not selling," BJ didn't even have to look at the amount. No amount could make her leave her family's business.

"Think about the offer. It's a good offer, very generous." He closed his briefcase. "I'll check back with you in a few days."

"No point, the answer will still be the same. You'll be wasting your time just like you're wasting your time now."

"We'll see." He lifted his chin and walked out of her bakery.

She could never sell. She had too many fond memories from her childhood of this bakery. It'd been updated a little over the years but the layout was still the same, all the way up to the apartment above. Her great-great-grandfather helped build the bakery. She had spent her afternoons doing her homework at the corner table by the window.

What would she do if she ever did sell the bakery? She'd never really thought about doing anything else. Baking was in her blood. What else was she good at? Only thing she'd ever really been good at was fishing. Maybe she would move down to the lake and become a fishing guide. BJ flipped the business card over looking at the back. Her eyes widened when she saw the amount. It was more than three times the value of the building. She would have plenty of money for a new place and plenty left over to buy a boat with all the bells and whistles. *Nope*, she shook her head. She was happy where she was. What would her customers do if they couldn't have her goodies every day? Mrs. Fields would have a fit. Tommy swears his wife can't get through her pregnancy without her chocolate eclairs. She wouldn't be going anywhere for a long time.

BJ pulled the cinnamon rolls out of the oven. The bell over the door rang out again. She expected to see Annette come in for her order of yeast rolls for the chef at the restaurant to try out. Instead, Gerri walked through the door with a smile on her face.

"Good morning, Gerri," BJ greeted her. "Would you like to try one of my cinnamon rolls? They just came out of the oven. They just need a little icing."

"Oh, that would be delightful. I'll take one to go." Gerri stepped up to the counter. "I found someone I'd like you to meet."

"Wow, that was fast," BJ commented. "I thought there would be a lot more to it."

She didn't think it would be this quick. The pounding in her chest almost turned to panic. She focused on applying the icing to the warm cinnamon rolls. Thoughts creeped in her mind, she was not ready to start dating again. BJ slowed her breathing, trying to calm down. She could feel Gerri looking at her.

"Sometimes it does take a while to find the right one. Then there are times when I can just sense things, and I sense he is what you need. He'll be good for you. I'd like to set up a date."

"Okay, under one condition. We meet at the restaurant at Heads N' Tails," she told Gerri. This way, Annette will be there in case she needed interference or an escape.

"That can easily be arranged," Gerri assured her. "I'll set it up and give you a call when I have details."

BJ placed one of the cinnamon rolls in a small to-go box and handed it to Gerri. Gerri pulled her wallet from her purse but BJ insisted it was on the house. A little cinnamon roll won't make or break her.

"Oh, I smell cinnamon rolls." Annette grinned as she came through the door. "Are they still warm?"

"Yep, just put the icing on." BJ took out another to-go box, knowing Annette wouldn't be leaving without some.

"Great, I'll take three. It's nice to see you this morning, Gerri." Annette turned toward Gerri.

"Have you tried a cinnamon roll? They're the best."

"Not yet, but I'm taking one with me." Gerri held up the box. "I have to go. I'll call you later BJ."

"Have a good day," BJ called out as Gerri was leaving.

"Did Gerri find you a man?" Annette waggled her eyebrows.

"Ugh, don't say it like that. It sounds creepy." BJ set a box up on the counter with three cinnamon rolls inside. "She says she found the one. Who knows?"

"Don't doubt her. If she said she found him, then I'd believe her." Annette opened the box and took a bite out of one of the cinnamon rolls. "Oh, that is so good," she moaned.

"Careful, you'll eat them all before you get back to the guys."

"Then I guess I'll have to come back for more. I do need to get going, though," Annette told her.

"Let me grab the rolls." BJ went to the small walk-in freezer. The cold air hit her as soon as she opened the door. A chill ran down her body when she stepped inside. She grabbed the two trays of yeast rolls she made yesterday.

"You're not scared you're going to get looked in there?" Annette asked peaking around the freezer door.

"No, the door has a stopper that prevents it from closing unless the handle is lifted." She nodded toward the stopper by the handle.

"I don't trust it," Annette admitted.

"Oh, it's fine." BJ closed the freezer door then set the trays of rolls on the counter. "I hope your chef likes them."

"Tobias will love them. I bet he'll want to order them weekly after one bite," Annette told her.

When Annette left, BJ knew she made the right decision. People loved her breads and pastries. To prove her thought, the morning rush began to come in five minutes later. She served her customers with a smile.

Four

Dare spent the morning sanding and staining the bar. Bryan had been installing light fixtures throughout the level. They would chat when Bryan would pass by, otherwise, it was all work. Dare knew how important it was for Bryan and Tony to get these levels done on time. Usually he'd work through lunch just to get ahead of the game. Bryan's phone rang out, echoing throughout the empty club level. Dare went about his business until he heard his name. He stood from his position behind the bar where he finished staining. Bryan was walking toward him, still talking on the phone. Bryan hung up before he knew what was going on.

"What's up?"

"That was Gerri." Bryan started texting, then looked up at him. "She wants you to meet her on the tenth level."

"On the tenth level? What for?" Dare hadn't been on that level yet.

"She didn't say what for, and the tenth level is just where she happens to be," Bryan answered.

"Now?" Dare looked at the bar. "This needs to dry anyway."

"See? It works out, now go." Bryan motioned toward the doors that led to the elevators.

Dare washed up before making his way to the elevators. Bryan stayed behind to finish his work. Last time Dare spoke to Gerri, she said she'd call. Why the sudden need to meet? He swiped his membership card and pressed the button for the tenth level. He wondered briefly about the type of club he'd find. Each floor was different from what Bryan had said. The familiar jolt from the elevator stopping snapped him from his thoughts. The moment the elevator doors opened, music pounded in.

Dare pushed open the door leading into the club. It wasn't exactly the type of place he thought he'd meet the older woman. He watched for a minute as an exotic dancer worked the pole. It amazed him to see such a small woman lift her body weight to do her pole tricks. Dare took his eyes from the dancer. He scanned the audience to look for Gerri. She sat at a table near the stage. Her short white hair stuck out like a beacon.

"Gerri." He nodded as he stepped up to the table. "I'm surprised you wanted to see me here."

"Dare, take a seat. Have a drink, the waitress will be back shortly," Gerri suggested.

Dare took a seat but wasn't interested in a drink at this hour in the morning. Instead, he waited for Gerri to tell him why she wanted to meet. However, she didn't speak, she watched the topless dancer swing around the pole. It wasn't until the dancer finished her routine that Gerri turned her attention to him.

"Such charisma in that one." Gerri nodded toward the dancer getting off the stage.

"I'm sorry, I don't understand what I'm doing here," he told Gerri.

"I wanted to see how you react to different women. If there's a certain type that attracts you. Such as the woman who was on stage."

"She's beautiful, but I prefer a woman that actually enjoys food," he told her honestly, and she laughed. "Plus, I'm old enough to be her father. I'd rather someone closer to my age."

"I'm glad to hear you say that because I think I have the perfect person in mind for you." Gerri smiled.

"If you had the perfect person in mind then what the hell am I doing here?"

"I needed to make sure I wasn't wrong." Gerri shrugged. "Plus, I told someone I'd stop by. Figured I'd kill two birds with one stone."

"Now that you're sure?"

"Now, I want to set you up on a date. Tomorrow night up at the restaurant on level eighteen. How's 7:30 for you?" Gerri asked.

"That's doable," Dare agreed.

"Good, reservations will be under Elwood. You know, I had one of the best cinnamon rolls this morning. You should stop by Bite my Bagel on your way to work in the morning. It's only nine blocks from here."

"It depends on what time I come in. I'll think about it though."

"Oh, you won't be let down I'm sure." Gerri winked at him then stood up. "I have to meet another client. I hope all goes well tomorrow night."

Gerri excused herself and left the table. Dare wasn't interested in sticking around for the show with all the work he had left to do. He went back to the twelfth level. He'd be able to get the clear coat on and start on the columns before he left for the day. He'd work late today to make up for the hour he'd take off early tomorrow.

****

The next morning Dare decided to stop by the bakery Gerri had mentioned. He worked right through dinner last night. When he had gotten home, he only had a small snack before falling asleep in his recliner. The small bakery was along the route he took to work every morning. He didn't know why he had never noticed it before. He parked his truck across the street from the bakery.

The bakery wasn't big compared to the other buildings in the area. The building had a historical look to it. The old window fronts gave it a welcoming feeling with pastries on display. A bell chimed above the door as he walked in. The warm scents of fresh bread reminded him of Saturday mornings. His stomach growled from the delicious smells. A woman came from the kitchen area carrying a tray of pastries. She slid the tray into a display case on the front counter.

"Welcome to Bite My Bagel. What can I get for you?" she asked with a slight southern drawl.

"I'll have two of whatever you just made."

"I just finished a batch of cannoli's and eclairs. My banana nut bread is still in the oven.

The cinnamon rolls are also fresh. They've only been on the shelf for half an hour."

"Tough one." He thought about his options. "I'll take a cannoli and a cinnamon roll. It smells delicious in here."

"It should, I've been here since five this morning." She smiled and fixed up a small box. She placed the pastries inside and set it on the counter in front of him. "Would you like something to drink with this?"

"Coffee please," he replied.

As she poured his coffee, he looked at the different pastries and chocolates she had on display. It was better than any bakery he had been to. This was more of a goody shop than a plain old bakery. She set his coffee cup beside the to-go box and rang him up. After paying, he wasn't in a rush to leave. Her smile had him drawn in like a mosquito to a bug light. She was beautiful. Her chestnut brown hair had strands of gray that shone like glitter when it caught the light from the window.

"You have a wide variety of sweets and breads," he commented.

"You have to have variety to stay in business these days. My grandfather only sold bread like generations before him. My mother added pies when she took over, and I added sweet treats to the mix." Suddenly, she closed her mouth. "I'm sorry, I seem to be rambling."

"You did well by adding the treats. I never realized this place was here," he commented, trying to stay in her presence just a little longer.

"It's been here for generations," she told him. "You just haven't been looking close enough."

"I won't overlook it again."

He needed to get to work, but he'd definitely be back. It wasn't until he was on the way to Heads N' Tails that he realized he didn't get her name. What he really wanted to do was cancel his date for tonight and ask out the woman at the bakery. Being a man of his word, he'd go on that date tonight. Without the promise of a second date, he could go back to Bite My Bagel and ask the baker out himself.

Five

BJ was wiping down the tables when Annette and Braelynn came bouncing in like youthful school girls. BJ admired their youthful energy.

"Put down the rag," Braelynn ordered. "It's time to get ready for your date."

"That's not until 7:30. I don't close the bakery for another hour," BJ protested.

"Not today." Annette flipped the sign to say closed. "Today you're going to let us treat you."

"For what? I'm not a girly girl," BJ admitted.

"You haven't been on a date in years. Let us do this for you," Braelynn pleaded.

"Fine, but I swear if you two try and put curlers in my hair I'll strangle you." BJ pointed at each one in turn.

"We promise, no curlers," Annette agreed.

"We have something better planned," Braelynn grinned. "Come on or we'll be late for our appointment."

"Appointment?" BJ questioned.

"I talked Ronan into getting us reservations at Cherise's Spa," Braelynn told her. "It's not a full complete body work up with a massage, but it's pampering none the less."

"You didn't have to do that."

"Oh, don't start thanking her yet," Annette laughed.

"I have a feeling I'm not going to like this." BJ grabbed her keys and left the bakery with Annette and Braelynn, locking the doors behind them.

On the way to the spa BJ tried prying information from Annette and Braelynn about what they had planned. She hated surprises of any kind. She'd rather know what she was getting into.

"It will be fun. We're all going to do it together," Braelynn said, pulling into the parking lot across from the spa.

"Let's get this over with." BJ got out of the car. "What's first on the agenda?"

"Waxing," Braelynn said as she held open the door to the spa.

"What?" BJ's eyes widened. "I barely have any hair on my legs as it is."

"It's not for your legs." Braelynn grinned. "Well, not just your legs."

"Oh, you've got to be shitting me!"

"It was all Braelynn's idea," Annette admitted with her hands up in surrender.

"Oh, I'm sure this is all her doing." BJ rolled her eyes as they approached the counter.

"Good evening, Mrs. Styles," a woman greeted Braelynn. "We have a room all set up for you lovely ladies."

"Thank you, Yvette." Braelynn looked back at BJ and winked.

"Just follow Vivian, and she'll get you all settled." Yvette motioned toward Vivian as she came closer.

Vivian led them to a room with three massage beds set up a few feet from each other.

White sheets covered each one, and pink robes were laid out across them. *Shit just got real,* BJ admitted to herself.

"We normally do this in separate rooms, on more comfortable beds," Vivian told them. "Undress at least from your waist down, put on the robes, and climb on the beds. All heads facing the center of the room."

"I can't believe I'm doing this," BJ said once Vivian walked out.

"Your date will love it." Braelynn unbuttoned her pants and pulled them off.

"Not tonight he won't." BJ kicked off her shoes. She slipped the robe on then stripped her pants and panties off.

"Is this about the guy from this morning?" Annette asked, changing into her robe.

"What guy?" Braelynn asked as they climbed onto the beds.

There was a knock on the door before BJ could answer Braelynn. The door opened and three women came in, each holding a tray of supplies. They instructed them on how to lay.

"The things I do for you girls." BJ's breath hitched when the cold cleaning spray touched her skin. "Never thought I'd be on a table with a woman between my legs other than my gyno."

The warmth of the wax wasn't as hot as BJ expected. She knew the time was coming to rip that sucker off and she wasn't looking forward to it. She closed her eyes and gritted her teeth.

"Whoa! What the fuck?" BJ yelled out as the first stripe was ripped off. "You two actually enjoy this?"

"It has its benefits," Annette laughed.

"It's torture, that's what it is." BJ took a deep breath and waited for the next strip to come off.

"Just relax," Braelynn insisted. "Tell me about that guy Annette mentioned earlier."

"There's nothing to tell." BJ shrugged. "I don't know anything about him, but damn, he was good looking. His eyes were glacier blue. His hair flowed passed his shoulders. A lot like Dave's hair was, but different colors."

"Maybe he'll come in again."

"What would I do with a man like that? He had to be in his early thirties at the latest. What would he want with an old broad like me?" BJ hissed as another strip came off.

"BJ, you still have a lot to offer," Annette told her.

"It doesn't matter, I didn't get his number. Hell, I didn't even get his name. All I can do is hope he comes in again. Besides, I have a date already."

"It's just one date," Annette reminded her.

"Consider it practice for when the man you really want pops up." Braelynn smiled through her own torture. "What are you going to wear?"

"I have some dresses you can look through," Annette offered.

"I'm not putting on a damn dress. That's not me, and I won't pretend it is. I have a nice outfit to wear."

Once their torture was over, they each got a manicure. Annette and Braelynn agreed to be at the restaurant having dinner at the same time as BJ's date. Though BJ was sure it was out of pure curiosity rather than being her back-up in case something went wrong.

They dropped BJ back off at the bakery. She went straight upstairs to her apartment. She still had plenty of time before her date. A long hot shower is what she needed. Hopefully, it would take away the sting from the torture session. Once she was out of the shower, she dried off and pulled out her pants outfit.

Before getting dressed, BJ put lotion on her legs. She had to admit her legs were smoother than she'd ever gotten by shaving. It would be a shame to cover her legs with pants. BJ went to her closet and flipped through her clothes until she came across a black skirt. She hadn't worn a skirt in years. She was surprised when it slipped easily over her hips. The skirt made her feel sexy. Now, she needed a shirt that made her feel sexy too. She had the perfect one in mind, a green silk blouse that showed off her cleavage. After checking herself out in the mirror, BJ left her apartment through the bakery.

****

BJ used the membership card Annette gave her to get to the restaurant at Heads N' Tails. The elevator ride up to the eighteenth level had her nerves rising. She wasn't nervous about going to the restaurant more about going on a date after years of being alone. Especially with someone she hadn't met before.

"Welcome to Heads N' Tails," the hostess greeted her. "How many?"

"I have a reservation under Elwood," BJ told her.

"The other member of your party has already arrived. Follow me." The hostess turned and led her through the restaurant.

BJ spotted Annette and Braelynn having drinks at a table near the bar. She hoped they would stay in view when she got to her table. The thought vanished the second she saw her customer from this morning sitting at a table looking straight at her. His lips were apart. Was the surprised look on his face good or bad? Earlier at the bakery, she thought he was into her. Now she wasn't too sure. Maybe she was just too old for him. As she approached the table, he stood up. He walked to the other side of the table and pulled a chair out for her.

"Thank you," she spoke softly as she sat down.

"It's a nice surprise to see you again." He sat down across from her. "I'm Darrow Forester. People just call me Dare."

"Betty Jean Elwood," she introduced herself. "I prefer to be called BJ though."

"BJ it is." He smiled.

A waitress came by and took their drink orders. BJ kept looking across the table at Dare as he looked over the menu. His hair hung low in his face. He caught her looking and smiled.

"I'm actually really surprised you're my date for tonight," BJ said honestly.

"Why is that?" he asked.

"To be honest, I was expecting someone older. More my age." She shrugged.

"I've been told I look good for my age." He smiled, flashing his pearly whites. "I'm not as young as you may think."

"How old are you then?" BJ asked.

"I'm only 53 years young."

"No, you're not!" BJ looked at him in disbelief. "You look to be in your early thirties. You're just trying to make me feel better."

"I swear it," he laughed. "Shifters age slower. It compensates for our longevity."

"Are you immortal?"

"No, just age slower than humans. I hope to still have 100 years left," Dare explained.

"Wow, I can't imagine living to be 150 years old."

"If I aged the way humans do, I wouldn't want to either."

The waitress came by with their drinks and took their food order. Conversation continued the moment she stepped away from the table. BJ couldn't believe her luck. What were the chances that he would walk into her bakery on the same day as their blind date with each other?"

"What made you come to the bakery this morning?" she asked him.

"Gerri told me about your amazing cinnamon rolls and suggested I stop for one," he told her.

"I figured Gerri had something to do with it," she admitted. "What is it you do for a living?"

"I'm a carpenter who specializes in wood carving. Right now, I'm working on the twelfth level of Heads N' Tails."

"Annette was talking about that one the other day. She said it should be open in a couple of weeks."

"That's the plan." Dare nodded. "I'll have to bring you by once all the carving is done."

"That'd be nice." She smiled, and her cheeks warmed. That meant he had to see her again.

"How do you know Annette?"

"I've known Annette since she was little. I used to babysit her and her friend Braelynn," she explained.

"I met Annette when Tony brought her in to see the place."

The waitress brought their food to the table. Conversation flowed as easily as a waterfall. They took turns telling each other a little about themselves. BJ stayed clear of mentioning Dave. Talking about her late husband would certainly kill the mood.

When their plates were cleared the waitress came back to take their plates, leaving a dessert menu on the table in their place. BJ wasn't ready for the night to end. It'd been a long time since she had enjoyed the company of a man. She looked over the menu, but kept thinking that once they were done with dessert the date would be over.

"You said my bakery was on your way home, right?" The question popped out before BJ had much chance to think about it.

"Yes, why?" he asked.

"Because I made a cheesecake that I'm dying to cut into."

"Cheesecake sounds perfect," he agreed. "I wouldn't want you to suffer any longer than you already have."

Dare paid the bill, leaving extra for a tip. He came around the table and pulled her chair out, offering his arm as she stood. On the way out, BJ looked toward Annette and Braelynn. They had massive grins and were giving her the thumbs up.

****

BJ drove back to her bakery. She glanced in her rearview mirror to make sure Dare was still behind her. Her stomach did flips the closer they got to her building. BJ parked in back in the small parking cove behind the buildings. She quickly got out and walked to the front. Dare parked in front of her bakery. He was getting out of his truck as she rounded the corner of the building. The streetlight lit up the front of her building, making it easy to unlock the door. Once they were both inside, she locked the door so no one would think the bakery was open.

"I'll get a pot of coffee going." BJ dropped her keys on the counter and turned on the lights in the kitchen area.

While the coffee was brewing, she went to the walk-in refrigerator to pull out the cheesecake.

She hadn't put on any toppings since Annette and Braelynn had her close early.

"What topping would you like? I have strawberry, blueberry, and cherry." She came out of the walk-in and placed the cheesecake on the counter.

"I've always been a sucker for strawberries." He stepped closer to her. "Is there anything I can do to help?"

"You can grab two plates." She pointed to the shelf above the coffeemaker.

She grabbed the strawberry topping from the walk-in refrigerator. Dare pulled two small plates from the shelf and set them by the cheesecake. BJ drizzled the strawberry topping on the cheesecake. As soon as the coffee pot finished brewing, Dare poured them both a cup of coffee while she cut two pieces of cheesecake and set them on the plates.

"Wow, that looks delicious." He handed her a mug.

"Wait until you taste it." She handed him a fork and took a bite of her own cheesecake. Dare took a bite and let out a moan.

"I believe this is the best cheesecake I've ever tasted," he commented.

"Thanks, I'm glad you like it." She sipped on her coffee then took another bite.

"You know I almost canceled our date tonight." Dare took a bite of his cheesecake.

"Why would you do that?" Her heart dropped.

"So, I could come in here and ask you out in the morning." He winked at her.

"Really?" Relief flooded over her.

"Yeah, I don't use dating services or anything like that ever. Bryan and Tony insisted I give it a try. Then when Geri suggested I come here. I knew the moment I saw you I wanted to ask you out. I would have done it then but I had this blind date."

"I hope your blind date didn't turn out too bad." She shoved a bite of cheesecake in her mouth to keep from saying something stupid. Instead, strawberry glaze dripped down her lip.

"I think it turned out great. Here, let me get that." Dare stepped closer to her.

He slowly wiped the glaze off her chin with his thumb. He moved in closer, bending down so he was on her level. His lips captured hers, taking the strawberry glaze from her lower lip. She didn't want the kiss to end. It seemed like forever since she'd been kissed. Her body melted into his as he deepened the kiss. It was a kiss unlike any other. It was a first kiss that beat all other first kisses. With that realization, her heart sank. Was this first kiss better than her first kiss with Dave? BJ slowly broke away from the kiss.

"Are you okay?" he asked as he wiped away a tear from her cheek.

"I'm sorry." BJ turned away quickly. She grabbed some napkins from the other counter while she got herself in check.

"It's okay, what's wrong?" His concern was written all over her face. "I thought the kiss was marvelous."

"It's not that." She sat the napkins by their plates. "Truth is I'm not in very good practice."

"Could've fooled me." Dare smiled at her.

"What I mean is, it's been over five years since I've kissed anyone." BJ hadn't planned on talking about Dave but since her emotions were leaving her no choice, she might as well spill it now. "I was married for 22 years."

"What happened? I'm assuming you aren't married anymore."

"No, I'm not. He died in a motorcycle wreck five years ago."

"I'm sorry, BJ." He took her hands. "If you're not ready to start dating again. I completely understand. Sarah, my late wife, died twenty years ago in a fire. Tonight, is my first date since. I understand your grief."

"I'm sorry to hear about Sarah. I guess we have more in common than I thought." She looked up at him.

"We can take things as slow as you would like." He wrapped his arms around her, holding her close.

"Thanks for understanding." She wrapped her arms around him and hugged him tight.

Dare helped her wash up the plates, then they sat down for another cup of coffee. They sat there and talked over coffee for another hour before Dare decided it was time for him to leave. He didn't try to push her into doing anything. He even asked her about Dave. She felt like she could tell Dare anything. BJ walked him to the bakery door. She knew he had to get sleep before work the next morning, but she didn't want him to leave. As he walked out the door, he turned back to her.

"Can I see you tomorrow?" he asked, taking her hand.

"I'd like that," she admitted.

He gave her a soft kiss before turning to go to his truck. BJ locked the door. She giggled like a schoolgirl on the way back to the bakery kitchen. She washed the mugs and went up to her apartment for a shower with hopes of hearing from Dare tomorrow.

Six

The next morning BJ danced around the bakery's kitchen while she made the morning's batch of bagels. She had a peaceful night's sleep with dreams of making love to Dare. She woke up with a smile on her face. All morning she had been humming and dancing while she did her morning routine. There was a knock on the glass door just as she put the pan of bagels in the oven. The bakery wouldn't open for another thirty minutes. She planned on telling the customer she wasn't open. That is, until she saw that it was Dare. Her smile grew instantly. She unlocked the door and Dare stepped in.

"I thought I'd swing by on my way to work." He bent down planting a kiss on her lips. "I couldn't wait to see you again. I hope it's okay I popped in like this."

"You can pop in anytime you want." BJ smiled and thought of the other ways to take that sentence. She locked the doors so other customers wouldn't come barging in. "Would you like a cup of coffee? I have some bagels in the oven but they won't be ready for another 20 minutes."

"Coffee will be great," he took her hand in his and they walked back to the kitchen.

"I'm glad you stopped by." She poured him a cup of coffee and refilled her own mug. "I wanted to ask you if you'd like to come over for dinner tonight."

"Of course, I'll come. I love your desserts. I can't wait to try your meals."

"No pressure there," BJ laughed.

"No pressure." He smiled. "What time should I be here?"

"What time do you get off work?"

"I can get off anytime. It's one of the perks to being my own boss. You just tell me a time and I'll be here."

"How about seven o'clock?" she asked.

"Sounds perfect," he agreed and drank the last of his coffee.

He checked the time on his phone and BJ knew he had to leave. She walked with him to the door, anticipating a goodbye kiss. She wasn't disappointed. Like the night before, when he got to the door he turned back. He took her in his arms and kissed her gently. His tongue teased her lips. She parted her lips, letting his tongue pass over hers. Her knees weakened as he wrapped his arms around her and deepened the kiss.

"You should be kissed like that every morning," Dare whispered against her lips as he broke away from their kiss.

"I'm glad you think so." She smiled up at him. "I think you should swing by every morning and see that it gets done properly."

"I plan on it." He gave a gentle peck on the lips. "Sadly, I have to go to work right now."

"I'll see you later then." She gave him another kiss then watched as he walked across the street to his pickup truck.

The timer rang out, echoing through the bakery. Her bagels were ready. She left the door unlocked and flipped her sign to say open. It was still too early for the morning rush, but it wouldn't matter if she opened a few minutes early.

****

After the morning rush, BJ pulled out her candy molds from under the prep table. She had an order for baby shower chocolates she needed to make today. Before she could pull the chocolate from the shelf, she noticed someone walking up to her bakery. She let out a long, exasperated sigh when she realized who it was. The bell above the door chimed as he came through the door. Irritation rose in her the moment he stepped into her bakery.

"What can I do for you, Mr. Jones?" BJ asked, coming out from the kitchen. "I highly doubt you came here for my bagels."

"I wanted to see if you've thought about my offer." He walked up to her sales counter with his briefcase in hand. She'd like to smack him in the back of the head with his own briefcase.

"I told you that you would be wasting your time if you came back." BJ crossed her arms. "The answer is still no."

"Your place doesn't belong here anymore. This building needs an upgrade to match the rest of the growing city."

"You know." She stroked her chin for affect. "I have been thinking about upgrading some of my displays. What do you think? Maybe a grand window display." She gestured widely with her arms.

"You'll lose your business soon enough. You'll be forced to sell when you can no longer pay your bills."

"My bills are no concern to you," BJ told him. The bell above the door chimed and Annette came in. "I assure you, Mr. Jones, this place will be open as long as people enjoy coming here for their pastries and delights."

Mr. Jones didn't say another word. He turned stiffly and walked toward the door. BJ rolled her eyes behind his back, then smiled at her friend. When Mr. Jones walked passed Annette, BJ saw her stick her foot out. Mr. Jones tripped over Annette's foot. He took a few hastened steps forward to gain his balance. As he opened the door, he turned toward her, placing his hand on the door jam.

"You'll change your mind." He paused and looked at his hand, then back at her. "Have a good day, Ms. Elwood." He turned and left her bakery.

"What was that all about?" Annette asked.

"He wants to buy the building. I'm guessing he hasn't heard the word 'no' much." BJ poured Annette a cup of coffee.

"Eh, he'll get over it." Annette shrugged. "If he keeps it up, report his ass."

"He hasn't done anything wrong," she sighed. "He is starting to annoy me though. He came in yesterday, too. Offered some obscene amount of money for the building. How'd Tobias like the yeast rolls?"

"Wow, subject change." Annette's eyes widened and she shook her head. "He absolutely loved them. In fact, he loved them so much he wants to order more."

"That's great." She could always use the extra business.

"Now, how much did he offer?" Annette asked, trying to steer the conversation.

"It doesn't matter because I said no. Let's talk about something else," she demanded.

"How did the date go last night? What'd you think of Dare?" Annette asked with a grin then sipped her coffee.

"Everything went well last night," BJ admitted. "He's a great guy."

"Did he dust off the old cobwebs?" Annette wagged her eyebrows.

"Annette!"

"What?" Annette raised her hands. "He's a good-looking guy. I saw how he looked at you. He was into you. Hell BJ, did you at least kiss the man?"

"Yes, we kissed," she admitted. "We're just taking things slow."

"Why?"

"I just... I don't know," BJ sighed. "We kissed last night and it felt like I was cheating on Dave."

"Please tell me you didn't run away."

"No, but I did tell him about Dave. He understands how I feel. He's been there before." She remembered him telling her of Sarah. "He's coming over tonight for dinner. I was thinking I would fix lasagna."

"You want me to get Bryan to tell him to leave early? I can," Annette offered.

"No, I need the time to close the bakery, cook, and shower."

"Okay, you know how to reach me if you change your mind. Let me get a few bagels before I leave." Annette eyed the bagels on display next to them.

"You're going back to Heads N' Tails, right?" She asked Annette as she put her bagels in a bag.

"Yeah, why?"

"I put an extra bagel in the bag. Will you drop it off for Dare?" She remembered his comment about trying her bagels. He had to leave before they came out of the oven.

"Yeah, I got you covered." Annette paid for her bagels and left the bakery.

Seven

BJ came out of the bathroom with a towel wrapped around her body and her hair dripping water down her back. She quickly glanced at the clock on the wall. She only had a little bit of time before Dare arrived. The smell of lasagna filled her apartment. She went to her bedroom to get dressed and wrap her hair in her towel. Thankfully, she didn't wear makeup, so getting ready only consisted of getting dressed and fixing her hair. She blow-dried her hair and brushed it straight. By the time she was done with her hair, the oven timer went off.

"Perfect timing," she said to herself going back into the kitchen.

She pulled the lasagna out of the oven and placed it on top of the stove to set. *Dare should be here any minute.* She grabbed the pan of garlic cheese bread and placed it on the middle rack of the oven then set the timer. Before she went downstairs, she took another look around her apartment to make sure everything was in place. Once she was satisfied with the way things looked, she went downstairs to the bakery. By the time she made it down the stairs, Dare was walking up to the bakery door. She quickened her steps to unlock the door for him.

"You're right on time." She opened the door for him.

"I try to never be late." He kissed her cheek and presented her with a bouquet of roses. "These are for you. A token of my appreciation for the delicious bagel."

"They're beautiful, thank you." She took a deep breath, inhaling the scent of the roses.

"What's on the menu tonight?" Dare took her hand in his as they walked through the bakery.

"Lasagna and garlic bread," she replied. "Oh, and I made a blueberry crostata for dessert."

"I've never tried a crostata."

"I think you'll like it. Oh shit, my bread." She raced up the stairs. When she opened her apartment door the timer on her oven was beeping. "Shit, shit, shit." She ran to the oven, opening the door.

"It will be okay. We don't need to have bread." Dare followed her into the kitchen.

"It's fine, not even burned." She pulled the pan out and set it next to the lasagna.

Dare grabbed both their plates from the table and handed her one. She cut them both a piece of lasagna, carefully transferring each piece to the plates. They each grabbed a piece of cheesy garlic bread before returning to the table.

"I have sweet tea, water, or diet soda," BJ told him as she opened the refrigerator.

"Sweet tea will be good." Dare brought the glasses over from the table and held them for her to pour the sweet tea.

"Dinner looks excellent." He sat the glasses back on the table and held out the chair for her.

"Thanks, I've been craving it for a week now. It's just too big of a meal for just one person." BJ watched as Dare took his first bite of her lasagna.

"I have to say, this is the best damn lasagna I've tasted." He took another bite. "I'm positive this beats Tobias' lasagna."

"There's plenty more where that came from." She bit into her cheesy garlic bread.

"Don't tempt me," he laughed. "I can eat that whole pan in one sitting."

When they finished dinner, Dare helped her wash dishes and put away the leftovers. BJ fixed him up a container with some leftovers for lunch the next day. She enjoyed feeding others. It was nice having someone to cook for.

"It's been a while since I've done the whole dating thing," she commented. "I wasn't sure what you would like to do, so I set out a few movies. Why don't you pick one of them?"

"Sure, point me in the right direction."

"They're set out on the coffee table. If you don't like any of those, there's a cabinet full of movies under the tv." BJ nodded toward the living room.

"I can handle that." He walked out of the kitchen then paused. "Do you mind if I light a fire in your fireplace?"

"Everything is right there. Matches are on the mantel." She put the dishes away.

She needed this moment alone. It's been a long time since she'd curled up with a man. Dave's favorite was watching the movie Ghost, while the fire flickered in the background. Maybe that's why she wanted to have dinner at her place. It was an impulse invite. She wanted to curl up and feel again. No one had sparked anything inside her until she met Dare. With Dare she could start to live again.

BJ went into the living room. She tried not to make any noise. If she did, he would move and she wouldn't be able to stare at his nice ass while he bent over to light the fire. Her heart pounded with the thrill of sneaking a look. His pants fit tight around his ass. For a moment, she wanted to walk over and get a handful. She smiled with her excitement. She thought she'd never get these feelings back. The flames started flickering, gradually getting bigger as the fire took hold.

BJ sat down on the couch, grabbing the remote off the coffee table. She turned on the tv and was taken back by the movie menu on the screen. She hadn't set this movie out.

"What made you pick Ghost?" she asked Dare as he sat down beside her.

"It's an awesome movie. I know it's not one you set out. We can switch it to something else if you would rather."

"No, it's fine," she told him. "I like Ghost, it just wasn't one I expected you to pick."

"It came close to being Die Hard, but something told me Ghost would be better." He laid back on the couch and pulled her to him.

She relaxed into him and started the movie. As the movie played, they got more comfortable. Dare took his boots off and propped feet up on the coffee table. BJ kicked off her shoes and brought her feet up on the couch next to her and laid across Dare's lap. He ran his fingers through her hair, twirling strands between his fingers. Halfway through the movie she changed positions again. Dare pulled her up so she was laying in his arms rather than his lap. Her body was pressed against his. A hard knot pressed against her arm. He had nipple rings. She licked her lips to cover her grin.

"Your heart's racing," Dare spoke gently.

"It's been a while." She was cut off by Dare's lips being pressed against hers.

She wrapped her arms around him, taking a fistful of his hair and deepened the kiss. He pulled her close, exploring her mouth with his tongue. She had almost forgot how much she enjoyed kissing. The movie played in the background, forgotten by both of them. She couldn't get enough of him.

A clang and clatter came from downstairs. BJ jumped from the sudden break in silence. The movie had ended and was back on the menu screen. She looked at Dare to see if he heard what she did. Another clatter had BJ jumping up and grabbing her baseball bat from behind the door.

"Where are you going?" Dare asked her when she opened her apartment door.

"I'm going to see who the hell is in my bakery, then I'm going to beat the shit out of them." She held her bat in a swinger's position.

"Hold on there, kitten." Dare placed a hand on her shoulder. "I'll go check it out. You stay here."

"Not a chance, I'm going down there." She took a step forward. Dare stopped her again and stepped in front of her.

"Fine, just let me go first." Dare quietly went down the steps, hoping to take them by surprise. When they reached the foot of the stairs, he flipped the lights on.

"Ah!" BJ screamed. "My bakery! This can't be happening."

Rats were scurrying around her bakery's kitchen like they owned the place. A lump in her chest formed at the sight of everything becoming contaminated by rodents. Tears insistently formed in her eyes. She'd never had a rodent problem, let alone a dozen rodents.

"I'll catch them," Dare told her. "Get something we can put them in. Something large with a lid."

"You're going to catch them?" BJ wasn't sure she heard him right.

"I'm going to try."

BJ ran back upstairs to her apartment. She closed the door behind her so none of the filthy rodents could easily run in. Frantically, she ran around her apartment trying to find something to use. She came across a large popcorn tin she had gotten for Christmas last year. She kept it to store her extra yarn in.

"This might work," she said opening the lid.

She dumped all the yarn out onto the floor and hurried downstairs. When she reached the bottom of the stairs, she expected to see rodents running amok. What she didn't expect to see was a humungous white Bengal tiger with its head under her prep table swatting at rodents with its paw. BJ missed the last step when she realized the tiger was actually Dare. The tin slipped from her hands, clattering to the floor. The tiger jumped, hitting his head on the bottom of the shelf under the prep table. BJ laughed when the tiger came out from under the table and looked at her. His eyes were wide like he had just been caught red handed. A rat hung by its tail dangling from the tiger's mouth and another was trapped under his paw. Carefully, he came over to the tin, sliding his paw with the rat underneath.

"Not exactly what I had in mind." BJ quickly scooped up the tin and opened it for him.

He dropped the rat from his mouth into the tin and grunted. BJ quickly covered it with the lid while he picked up the other rat with his teeth. While he dropped it into the tin, she looked for others.

"There," she pointed at another rat running along the edge of the sales counter.

The tiger crouched down, stalking his prey. With a wiggle of his tail, he pounced on the rat, trapping it under his paws.

"Yes!" She quickly ran over to him. He picked the rodent up with his teeth and dropped it in the tin.

They hunted rodents for half an hour. BJ mostly spotted and pointed out the rats and Dare did all the catching. It was strange that he caught them in his mouth, but since he was a tiger it didn't seem so gross. Better him than her, she shivered when he dropped the last one in the tin. The scurrying of the rodents inside the tin gave her the creeps. She put the tin down on the table, glad to get it out of her hands.

"I don't know how they could have gotten in here," BJ said to herself.

"They were put here," Dare startled her.

"You're a tiger!" She watched intently as he rearranged his shirt.

"I am?" His eyes widened like he didn't know then he burst out laughing. "The look on your face was priceless."

"No, the look on your furry face was priceless when you had that rat hanging out of your mouth," BJ laughed.

"Not my favorite moment." His face scrunched up in disgust.

"You were adorable." She brushed his hair over his shoulder.

"I'm a tiger, we don't do adorable." Crossing his arms, he looked serious but it came off as more of a pout.

"Adorably ferocious?" Taking his hands, she unraveled his arms and stepped into him. Placing his arms around her, she hugged him.

"I like ferocious." His arms tightened around her.

"Let's tape this top down so they don't get out." BJ grabbed the tape from under the sales counter and ran a strip around the tin.

"How could someone put them here? The door has been locked." BJ pushed on the door to show him it was locked. The door gave way under her weight. She almost fell out the opening door but Dare grabbed her hand.

"You may have locked it, but it's not locked anymore," Dare commented.

BJ righted herself and looked at the door. That's not possible. She had the only key to the building. She pulled the door closed and turned the lock. The familiar click sounded letting her know the door was locked.

"I locked this door before we went upstairs," she told Dare. "I'm sure of it."

Dare came over to her and pushed on the locked door, it easily swung open.

"How the hell?" BJ asked in disbelief.

Dare stepped in front of her, looking at the door lock. With the door opened, he twisted the lock. The bolt came out as it should. He turned his attention to the door jam.

"Someone blocked the lock," he told her, pointing to the door jam.

"What is that?"

"It looks like some type of expansion foam," he told her.

"How? Who? Why?" she asked, still in disbelief.

"The only reason I can see behind putting rats in a food place is to have them shut down."

"That's it." She snapped her finger. "That slimy piece of shit, he did this."

"Who?"

"Mr. Jones." She took out her phone to call the cops. "He works for McNeilsons. They want to buy this place, and I'm not selling."

Dare pulled out his pocket knife and popped holes in the tin lid. They waited for the police to show up but not much was accomplished. Everything had been wiped down. They pulled some prints from the door, but BJ believed they'd turn out to be hers. She told them her suspicions about Mr. Jones, but without surveillance it was hard to prove. Dare agreed to take the rats out to the state park on his way home.

"I can fix the lock," Dare told her once the police left. "I have to run out to the truck. I'll be right back."

"Thanks." She appreciated all his help. How would she have caught all those rats by herself?

At least they were able to catch them all. She'd have to bleach everything tonight, but she'd be able to open in the morning. She walked around the bakery checking the floors and under the tables. Dare came back in with a chisel and hammer. Movement caught the corner of her eye, she looked to the display against the wall. A rat was helping itself to her muffins.

"Dare, do you think you can catch that one too?" She pointed to the display.

"Pull the tape off the lid." He put the hammer and chisel down on the floor by the door.

Dare slowly made his way around the sales counter and to the back of the display. The rat was trapped in the display with only one way out. Dare made it look easy to quickly reach his hand in and snatch up the rat. The rat squealed out and flopped around in his hand. BJ rushed the tin over to him. Once the rat was inside, she added more tape around the lid.

"I'll do another sweep while you finish with the door." She began her search again.

Dare was still chiseling the hardened foam out of the lock hole when she finished the search. With the rat in the food display, there was no way she could open tomorrow. She pulled out the large trash can from the kitchen and began tossing everything from the displays. She couldn't take the chance of anything being contaminated.

"This is what he wanted." She forcefully threw the muffin in the trash. "He wants me to close. If I don't have any goods, then I can't make any sales. It's going to take me all night to bleach everything."

"It'll only take you half the night if I help," Dare offered. He closed the door and locked it, giving it a push to make sure it was truly locked.

"I couldn't ask you to do that."

"You didn't, I offered." He came over to her and wrapped her in a hug. "Plus, I wouldn't be able to sleep knowing you're scrubbing this place all night."

"I wouldn't want you to lose sleep because of me." She gave him a squeeze. "First, I insist on us going upstairs and having our dessert."

"If you insist, then I can't deny you."

After dessert, BJ put on some music and they bleached every surface in the bakery. It took them two hours when they tackled it together. They kept an eye out for any more rodents that may be running around. Luckily, they didn't come across any.

"Man, this sucks ass." BJ dropped her rag into the sink. "I still can't open tomorrow. I'll be lucky if I can open on Saturday. Sorry, this wasn't an ideal date."

"It's okay." Dare dropped his rag on top of hers and took her in his arms. "I got to spend time with you. It doesn't matter what we do. I'll come by on later and help you bake. I can't promise It will be perfect, but I can follow directions."

"Don't worry about it. I know you have to work. You can swing by afterwards if you want."

"I'll be here by seven and pick up some dinner on the way over," he offered.

"Good, I don't think I'll want to cook after all the baking I'll be doing." She never felt like cooking when she had a big baking day.

"I'm going to get those rats out of here. I'd kiss you but I'd like to brush my teeth first."

"You can make it up to me tomorrow." She smiled.

Dare grabbed the tin on his way to the door. BJ held his hand and walked him to the door. She really wanted to kiss him but the thought of rats hanging from his mouth kept her in check. He pulled her in for a hug when he got to the door. She buried her face in his neck, kissing his skin.

"I'll see you tomorrow," she said as he walked out the door.

"Later, kitten." He smiled back at her as he crossed the street.

She locked the door, pushing on it to make sure it locked. Confident no one could come in, BJ went upstairs calling it a night. Thankfully the place was clean because she was utterly exhausted. She locked her apartment door behind herself and stripped her clothes off on the way to her bed. It only took a minute for her to fall asleep.

Eight

All morning BJ had been baking and turning away customers. Even being closed for one day was seriously going to hurt business. She had printed out coupons to offer to her customers in hopes of bringing them back. She'd make one batch of everything in order to open in the morning. She dropped some blueberries into the muffin mix when someone tried to open the bakery door. BJ went to the door, grabbing a couple coupons off the table.

"You're opening late today BJ," Peggy spoke when BJ opened the door.

"I'm not opening today, Peggy." She handed Peggy the coupons. "I should be open in the morning. Come back and get a free sweet treat."

"Oh no, what happened?" Peggy asked taking the coupons.

"Busted pipe," BJ lied.

"I hope there's not much damage."

"No, it's a good thing I live here. I was able to catch the problem quickly."

"Good, I'll swing back by on my way home from work tomorrow."

Peggy turned and continued down the sidewalk. Before BJ turned to go back inside, she noticed Mr. Jones standing on the sidewalk across the street. Anger built in her, his smug face told her everything. He did it, and she knew it. She tossed the leftover coupons onto a table just inside the door and stormed across the street. He stood there with a smile on his face. She was going to wipe that smile off his face. Without saying a word, she balled up her fist. She swung, connecting with his lower lip. He stumbled back but corrected himself before falling.

"Careful, Ms. Elwood. You wouldn't want to catch an assault charge." He wiped the corner of his mouth with a handkerchief from his jacket pocket.

"You did this." She pointed at him.

"I'm afraid I don't know what you're talking about. How's business going?" he asked with a smirk. "I see you haven't opened yet. Is there a problem?

"Don't play dumb with me. You put those things in my bakery last night."

"If what you say is true, where's your proof? You must have some." He knew she'd have nothing against him.

"Stay the hell away from my business. You won't be getting your slimy hands on my building." She turned and went back to her bakery.

She wanted to punch him again but she'd be lucky if he didn't press charges on her now. The nerve of him to come and watch what he caused. She gritted her teeth and held her hands tight beside her to keep herself in check. It took everything she had not to go back over there and beat him. It's one thing to want to buy her place but he crossed the line when he tossed rats into her bakery. Karma would catch up with him. Somehow, he would get caught.

For right now, she needed to take her mind off things. Her blueberry muffins just needed to be scooped into the muffin pans, and her cookies were ready for their icing. She made special cookies for coupon holders in honor of Dare and all his help. There was still plenty she had to make.

****

BJ slid a batch of cupcakes into the oven and set the timer. There was a knock on the door, and excitement ran through her. She peered out from the kitchen to see Dare at the door holding a pizza box. She tossed her rag onto the counter and went to unlock the door for him.

"I'm glad to see you." She gave him a hug when he set the box down on the table.

"Kitten, what happened to your hand?" he asked, taking her right hand in his. He kissed her swollen hand.

"Mr. Jones needed to be brought down a peg."

"He was here?"

"Not exactly." She looked up at him. "He was across the street."

"Maybe I should have a chat with Mr. Jones," Dare suggested as she locked the door.

"I don't want you to get into any trouble. It would be worse on you because you're a shifter and he's a human." She stood on her tip toes and pressed her lips against his. "Mr. Jones will get caught. You have to have faith in that."

"I'd have more faith if I had a little talk with him," Dare insisted and grabbed the pizza box

"He'll give up once he realizes I'm not selling." She led him to the back of the bakery where she had a table set up for them to have dinner.

"I didn't know what type of pizza you like, so I took a chance and got a meat-lovers." He opened the box exposing the pizza.

"My favorite." She pulled a piece out and placed it on her plate.

She ate a slice before the oven timer went off. Her stomach growled in protest as she stepped away from the table to get the cupcakes out of the oven. The medium pizza didn't last long once she got back. BJ had been baking all day and only had a muffin for lunch. She crushed up the pizza box and took it to the kitchen trash. She pulled out a couple of cookies she made early and placed them on a napkin. She wanted Dare to be the first person to try one.

"Bite my Bengal." She held one out to him.

"You can bite my Bengal," he teased, taking the cookie from her. "This is creative, it looks just like me."

"Well, that was the plan. Think of it as a thank you for saving my bakery." She kissed his cheek.

"You're more than welcome." He took a bite of the sugar cookie.

It was in the shape of a tiger's head. She decorated it with white and black icing to match his tiger. Each cookie had blue eyes just like his. Without him, she wouldn't be able to open her bakery tomorrow.

"What are we fixing first?" he asked pushing away from the table.

"I still have to make a cake and another batch of cupcakes. When they cool, we can add the icing." She told him, grabbing their plates and bringing them into the kitchen.

"Just tell me what to do." He rubbed his hands together.

"First, wash your hands."

Over the next hour, they were able to get all her planned baking done. They both mixed batches at the same time. It saved time having some help. While the cakes cooled, she started piping the icing onto the cupcakes. Dare put them in the small cupcake container and she came behind him piping the icing on top. Once the icing was on, Dare would come behind her and add sprinkles to some.

"Pick a color for the cake decorations." She smoothed white icing onto the cake and added a layer.

"Green, like your eyes," he answered without hesitation.

She piped on the green icing, while he moved the packaged cupcakes to the display case. He couldn't possibly understand the appreciation she had for his help. It meant the world to her. She lost her train of thought for a moment when he walked past her with cupcakes. Her piping missed the cake, landing on the edge of the base. She scooped the icing up from the base and waited for him to pass again.

"Is this the right shade of green?" she asked, getting his attention. When he turned to her, she wiped the icing on the tip of his nose. He smiled and swiped his finger through the glob of icing on his nose.

"I think this color looks better on you." He reached out and wiped it down her cheek.

Her eyes widened with surprise. Since she didn't need anymore of the icing, she might as well have a little bit of fun with it. She dipped her finger in the icing bowl, getting a glob on her fingertip. He tried to dance out of her way, but she managed to swipe his cheek. He moved in between her and the bowl, dipping his finger inside.

"Two can play at that game." He turned to her with icing on both his index fingers.

BJ let out a playful squeal and ran out of the kitchen. Dare chased her around the bakery. They both laughed as they weaved around the table. He caught her at the steps that led up to her apartment. She spun around, and they both fell to the steps laughing. Dare wiped icing on her cheek and down her neck.

"Damn, I made a mess." He grinned at her. "I guess I'll have to clean that up."

He pressed his lips against the icing on her cheek. She leaned her head back, letting him slowly lick the icing from her neck. His lips were warm against her skin. She wanted more. She should have more. She pulled him to her and he kissed her lips. His tongue was sweet from the icing. Her hands went to his shirt, fiddling with the buttons. One came undone and she moved to the next. He stopped kissing her and look into her eyes.

"What are you doing?" He grinned.

"I think we should take this to the next level." She smiled and the second button came undone.

He smiled and pressed his lips against hers. She unbuttoned another button as he wrapped his arms around her and lifted her up. Clearly, he had the strength to hold her up, but she wrapped her legs around him anyway. He carried her up the stairs with his hands on her ass. She nuzzled her face in his neck, lightly scraping her teeth along his neck. A growl came from deep within him, sending a satisfying chill down her back. She did that to him. When they got to the top landing, she reached behind her and twisted the doorknob. Dare carried her through and kicked the door shut.

Without a pause, he took her straight to her bedroom. He didn't give her time to reach for the light switch. With the bedroom door open, the light from the living room lit up a trail to the bed. He gently laid her down on the bed.

Her legs tightened around him as she leaned up, stripping off his shirt. His body was in shape and well defined. Her fingers splayed out along his muscular chest. Taking in the wonderful view before her, she bit her lip. She loved nipple rings. She leaned forward, taking one into her mouth. Her tongue flicked over the small ring. She couldn't keep her hands off of him as the heat built within her.

"Are you sure you're ready?" he asked her softly.

Not trusting her voice, she nodded. She pulled him down on top of her, claiming his lips. His passionate kiss warmed her soul. He tugged her t-shirt out of her jeans. She raised her arms, allowing him to pull her shirt over her head. He kissed his way down her shoulder, sliding his hand behind her. She arched her back to give him room. With a quick flip of his hand, her bra sprung forward under the weight of her breasts. He leaned back pulling her bra off as he went. His abs clenched as her fingers tugged on his zipper. He unbuttoned her jeans and pulled them down her legs taking her panties with them. He stepped off the bed and stripped off his pants. His hardness sprung forth from its confines.

He climbed back onto the bed and positioned himself in front of her. His fingers danced down her skin, sending thrilling chills down her body. She arched her body into his touch. With every touch she felt more alive. His hand slipped over her apex. It was then she felt her own heat against his hand. His finger circled over her clit, making her body quiver. With a quick dip, his finger slipped inside her. He bit his lip and smiled.

"You're wet for me already," he commented, sliding his finger out and around her clit again. "Mmm, you're so ready."

He licked his lips and leaned down, placing a gentle kiss on her belly. His soft lips grazed her skin as he made his way to her core. She held her breath as his lips came down upon her clit. His tongue darted out, flicking across her clit. Her body reacted to him immediately, jerking with every flick of his tongue. He dipped a second finger inside her, stretching her opening. She wasn't going to be able to handle much more of his teasing.

"You're not going to make a woman wait, are you?" She asked as he sat up.

"Not a chance, kitten." He pulled her legs up and around him as he positioned himself between her thighs.

He teased her entrance without entering. His shaft slid easily between her folds. Her core throbbed with anticipation. She lifted her hips, guiding him into her. He pulled out then plunged deep inside her. He filled her completely, stretching her to the fullest. She moaned out in pleasure. She lifted her hips, meeting him with every thrust. Her hands splayed out on his chest, exploring his body. She lifted herself and took his nipple ring into her mouth. She tugged with her teeth and flicked the ring with her tongue. His hands came around to her ass and squeezed her cheeks. With each thrust he lifted her to him.

She cried out in pleasure as he brought a finger to her forbidden spot. Without entering, he pressed his finger down and massaged her. It gave her a feeling she'd never had before. She moaned in ecstasy. The harder he pounded into her the more pressure his finger applied. Her body pulsed as she came closer to climax with each thrust. Her legs tightened around him as her core muscles tightened around his shaft. Her orgasm exploded within her. She called out his name as she rode out her orgasm. Years of pent up sexual aggression spewed out of her with each of his continued thrusts. His body shuddered from his release as he thrust deep inside her. His cock throbbed as his cum filled her. With one last thrust, he pulled out from her.

He collapsed down beside her and pulled her to him. She laid against his chest and played with his nipple ring, flipping it from one side to the other. Her body weaken, she laid against him. Never had she felt that complete.

"I have to go put everything away downstairs." She patted his chest and got up.

"No cuddling?" he teased and playfully smacked her rear when she turned from him.

"It won't take me long, then I'll come back and cuddle," she assured him with a smile.

"I'll come help. That way we can get back up here quicker." Dare got up from the bed.

"Alright, let's wash up and get to it." She left the bedroom and went into the bathroom.

Thirty minutes later they were laying back down in the bed. The day's toll started weighing in on her. Thoughts of their love making left her heart feeling torn. Her feelings for Dare were growing, leaving her feeling guilty. Even though Dave was no longer there, she still felt like she cheated on him with Dare. Her eyes grew heavy with guilt nagging at her. She fell asleep in Dare's arms thinking about the world of trouble her heart was in.

Nine

BJ woke up early the next morning, still in Dare's arms. Panic began to set in the longer she laid there. It'd been a long time since she spent the night in a man's arms. Guilt set in over her panic. She slid from the bed careful not to wake him. *This was a mistake. What would Dave say?* She quietly grabbed her clothes from the dresser and ran into the bathroom. She'd jump in the shower then go down to the bakery.

After her shower she braided her hair before leaving the bathroom. She slowly opened the bathroom door, not wanting to wake Dare. Her shoes were still in the bedroom. She tiptoed into the room, and found her shoes by the foot of the bed.

"Running off this early?" Dare opened his eyes and looked straight at her.

"I wasn't running off." She stood with her shoes in hand. "It takes damn near three hours to make bagels, give or take depending on type. I need to get an early start if I want to be prepared for my customers."

"This is about last night." He sat up in the bed. "I know how it feels, with this being your first relationship since Dave. It's okay to feel guilty." He got up from the bed and gave her a hug. "Dave would want you to be happy. For now, I'm going to go and let you come to your own conclusions."

"Thanks for being understanding." She wrapped her arms around him. "I'll call you later."

He softly kissed her lips then gathered his clothes. She put on her shoes and walked down the stairs. Dare had been more understanding than she thought he would be. He's been in her situation. He knew better than anyone how it feels to lose a lover. When she came down into the bakery, the first thing she did was start a pot of coffee. While Dare was getting ready, she fixed him up a breakfast bag. When her apartment door opened, she knew Dare was coming down. She poured him a cup of coffee and set it by the bag.

"At least you're sending me off with sustenance." He walked over to the coffee and bag. "Is this one mine?" He pointed to the coffee by the bag. BJ nodded as he picked it up and took a sip.

"I'm not sending you off. Really, I'm not." She didn't want him to think that she didn't want to see him anymore because that's the opposite of what she really wanted. She just had to come to terms with things first.

"I know, kitten." He kissed her forehead. "Call me when you're ready. Remember what I said. He would want you to be happy."

She leaned against the counter and watched him leave the bakery. He was right, Dave would want her to be happy. She's pretty sure if Dave was still alive, he could actually be friends with Dare. They had a lot in common. Dave had a fascination with wood carving but was never able to get the detailing down. He would have picked Dare's brain for tips and pointers. BJ nodded to herself. Dave would have approved of Dare. If Dave could have hand picked someone for her, it would be Dare. The realization made her heart a little lighter.

It was back to business as usual. She had just finished with the bagels when it was time to open. Even being closed for only one day, BJ could tell it did a number on her customers. Today, she barely had half her normal customers. The morning rush couldn't even be called that today. She was only closed for one day.

"I just don't get it," BJ sighed as she wiped down the sales counter.

It was one day, and anybody that had asked she told them it was plumbing. *So why were her customers not back? Madison always came in by this time.* The bell above the door rang out, as Mrs. Pearly came in with her granddaughter.

"Good morning, Mrs. Pearly," BJ greeted then looked down at the bright little girl skipping in beside her. "Wow, Suzie! You've gotten tall since I saw you last."

"I'm gonna be four." Susie held up her fingers.

"Yes, her birthday is this weekend," Mrs. Pearly confirmed. "I thought I'd bring her by for a cupcake. You're not as busy as usual."

"Not today," BJ agreed. "What color cupcake would you like Susie?"

"That one," Susie pointed out a cupcake with green icing and sprinkles.

"Excellent choice." BJ smiled at Susie as she pulled the cupcake from the display case.

"I'll take one as well," Mrs. Pearly commented before she closed the display. "You know I have a theory on your lack of customers."

"Oh, what's that?" BJ rang up their order.

"I was down at the market on Gaines St. I overheard a woman telling people that you had a rat infestation. Can you believe that?"

"Mrs. Pearly, I assure you there are no rats here." BJ told her. *How did someone know?*

"Don't you worry, dear. I didn't believe it for a second. This place has always been in tiptop shape, if you ask me. That's why you have an A rating hanging in the window." Mrs. Pearly handed her cash.

"Gammy got mad." Susie's eyes widened.

"She did?" BJ looked over the counter at Susie.

"Well, that woman was saying horrible things," Mrs. Pearly justified. "I can't help it if my mouth kind of got away from me. It's hard to bite your tongue these days. With the lies people spread around, not caring who it hurts. It's a shame, I tell you."

"I appreciate you standing up for the bakery like that."

"It wasn't just for the bakery, dear. It was for you, too. I've been coming here for many years. Since before you were born actually. I couldn't stand to see someone try and run you into the ground."

"Thanks, here take these." BJ took out two Bengal cookies.

"Pretty tiger." Susie noticed the design as BJ slid the cookies into the bag.

"Thanks, dear." Mrs. Pearly held Susie's hand with one and the bag of goodies in the other. "I'll see you next week."

"Have a wonderful weekend," she told Mrs. Pearly. "Happy early birthday, Susie."

"Thanks." Susie opened the door for her grandmother, and they walked out of the bakery.

BJ went back to the kitchen and started the dough mixture for cinnamon rolls. She started the mixer up adding ingredients for a small batch. She didn't want to waste ingredients in case her normal customers didn't come back by tomorrow. The bell over the door rung and a woman came in holding a little boy's hand. The little boy was jumping and trying to pull away from his mother.

"Welcome to Bite My Bagel," BJ greeted her. "What can I get for you two?"

"I need a blueberry muffin for me and a banana nut muffin for Johnny," the woman said politely.

"Sure, would you like something to drink with that also?"

"I'll have a water and whatever type of juice you have for my son." The woman reached into her purse for money and her son tried to run off. She snatched him back by his hand and told him to wait.

BJ grabbed their order and placed it in a bag, then grabbed the bottled water and juice. She set everything on the counter and rang her up. The woman gave the juice to her son and they sat at the table by the window near the kitchen. BJ hoped that people would see them through the window and stop in. BJ went back into the kitchen to pull the dough out of the mixer. It would need to rise for an hour, so she went to the walk-in cooler for ingredients to make some tarts. She walked to the back for the blueberries and without warning, the walk-in cooler door slammed behind her.

"Hey!" BJ dashed to the door. She beat on the cold metal door. "Open the door."

"Come on Johnny, let's go." BJ heard the woman through the door, but she sounded closer than the table they were sitting at.

"Wait, let me out!" BJ yelled and banged on the door. "I can't get out!"

She heard laughter getting farther away. The bell over the door was hard to hear through the thick door. She couldn't hear any laughter or the rambunctious boy running around. She was alone in her bakery.

"Damn it," she kicked the metal door.

She reached into her back pocket for her phone. Unlocking her phone was useless. She didn't have any service through the 5-inch walls of steel and insulation. At least she wasn't in the freezer. She didn't want to push the shut off button because it would only shut of the power not open the door. This was what she got for fixing this old model rather than getting a new walk-in cooler. She'd definitely spring for the freezer and cooler after this. She pounded on the door again but it was for nothing since no one was in the bakery with her.

She heard the faint bell, as someone came into the bakery. She pounded her fists on the door. There was no response. She yelled out for them to open the door but still there was nothing. *Maybe no one came in.* She gave up trying to get someone's attention. She heard the faint bell again. Someone was in there. They probably cleaned out the register. Luckily, she didn't have many customers throughout the morning.

She rubbed her arms with her hands to take the chill off. The longer she was in there, the colder she got. *How long before hypothermia set in?* When her teeth started chattering, she became worried. She almost missed the sound of the bell above the door. Someone was in the bakery. She pounded on the door, hoping that someone would let her out.

"Please, open the door!" she yelled out.

"BJ?" She recognized Annette's voice.

"Annette, open the cooler," she called out. A moment later, Annette opened the door. BJ quickly stepped out of the cooler. She grabbed her sweater off the back of the stool and put it on. She checked the register to see if she'd been robbed, but all the cash was still in the register's till.

"I thought you couldn't get stuck in there?" Annette crossed her arms. "I thought you said those doors couldn't close on their own."

"They can't, someone helped them out."

"You mean someone closed you in there on purpose?" Annette's eyebrows scrunched together.

"Yes, someone had to lift that handle in order to close the door. It wasn't an accident." She was sure the woman had shut her in there. "Someone else came in while I was in there, but nothing seems to be missing. Maybe they didn't hear me banging on the door. Thankfully you stopped by. Why are you here?"

"Unless they were deaf, they heard you. I could hear you from the entrance. As far as why

I'm here. Dare asked Bryan to see if I'd stop by and check on you. Which has me wondering, why you needed to be check on." Annette eyed her. "What's going on?"

"Nothing, he's just giving me a little space," she said honestly.

"Space from what? You two are just getting started."

"I know, and he's the greatest," BJ sighed.

"So, what's the problem?"

"The problem is, I feel guilty," she told Annette. "If I was ready to move on, I wouldn't feel guilty."

"You're always going to love Dave. There's no denying that. But girl, he's no longer here and you have so much life left. Too much to be alone the whole time."

"I know, and I'm working through it," she admitted with a sigh.

"He likes you a lot. I wouldn't keep him waiting too long," Annette suggested and grabbed a cupcake from the display.

"I'll give him a call later," she agreed.

"Good, I think you two are brilliant together." Annette gave her a hug. "I have to go. I have an appointment at the spa."

"You're going back to the torture chamber?" BJ asked, remembering the way the hardened wax ripped from her skin.

"Not today," Annette laughed. "Call me if you need me. Try to stay out of the cooler."

"Hey, don't say anything about that. I'll tell Dare when he comes over."

"Suit yourself." Annette waved as she walked out the door.

BJ checked the door to the cooler. There wasn't a malfunction. Everything was working properly. She even put her body weight against the door to see if it would close without lifting the handle. Nothing, you still had to lift the handle. It was just as she thought, someone shut her inside the cooler on purpose.

Ten

Dare was surprised when BJ called and asked him to come over. He didn't expect to hear from her for a few days. The look on her face this morning told him she wasn't ready for a relationship. He saw the panic in her eyes when she was trying to snatch her shoes and run. He understood what she was going through. He'd been there. After Sarah died, he didn't want to date anyone again. After twenty years of being alone, it got lonely. He didn't want to rush BJ or push her into anything before she was ready. For the first time since Sarah died, he found someone he enjoyed spending time with. He didn't want to mess that up by rushing their relationship on her. He'll wait until she was ready.

He promised to swing by the bakery after work. Bryan mentioned that they'd be hanging out on level fifteen tonight. Bryan asked if Dare wanted to bring BJ up there since Annette and Braelynn would be there too. Before leaving, he used one of the rooms to get cleaned up.

When he arrived at BJ's bakery, it was already closed. All the lights were out except for the one in the kitchen. He could see BJ through the glass door. She looked up, and smiled the most beautiful smile he'd ever seen. She had taken the braids out of her hair, leaving it slightly curly. Her hair swayed as she walked to the door to unlock it. He'd like to wrap her hair around his hand and kiss her until she forgot about everything else.

"Hi, I'm glad you came." BJ gave him a tight hug, one he wasn't expecting.

"I'm glad you called." He could sense something was bothering her. "Is something wrong?"

"Not anymore. I wanted to thank you for sending Annette by. I'd probably still be stuck in the cooler if you didn't."

"What? How'd did that happen?" It was too much of a coincidence that she got trapped in her cooler the same week as the rat incident.

"I think a woman shut the door when I went in for the blueberries."

"Did you see her?" he asked, hoping she could identify her.

"I didn't see her do it, but her and her son were the only ones in the bakery. I screamed to be let out. I heard the woman, so I know she heard me. Someone else came in the bakery while I was trapped. They didn't open the door for me, but they didn't take anything either."

"Maybe they didn't see anyone, so they left," he suggested.

"I guess, but they stayed a little too long for that. You can barely hear the bell from inside the cooler but you can still hear it. I think they should have heard me. Annette heard me just fine."

"At least you're okay." He took her hand as they walked toward the kitchen. "You need a security system, one with cameras on the inside and out."

"I've already taken care of that. Everything will be installed on Monday. I was wondering if you could build a half door to go here, just the bottom part." She indicated the high counter that separated the kitchen from the rest of the bakery.

"Kitten, I can make you anything you want. Would you like something carved into it?" he asked thinking of ideas.

"Something pretty but not girly," she didn't hesitate.

"Got it, no hearts and flowers. I need to run out to my truck and get my measuring tape. I'll be right back."

He went out to his truck while she waited by the door. He ran back across the street to the bakery. BJ held open the door then locked it once he was inside. It wouldn't take him long to get the measurements he needed. He knelt down beside the counter and started taking the measurements then put the results in his phone. BJ leaned up against the sales counter behind him.

"You know, I happen to know for a fact that two of your best friends will be at Heads N' Tails tonight. I was thinking maybe you would like to go out and grab a drink?"

"After the last couple of days, a drink sounds great." She squeezed passed him and headed for the stairs. "I'll go get ready. Trust me I won't be long."

He didn't think she would. It was one of the things he liked about her. She was natural. If she was wearing any makeup at all, he couldn't tell. To him, she was still more beautiful than the models on tv. Her hair wasn't unnaturally colored. She let the gray strands grow where they willed. He finished the measurements and waited for her downstairs. A couple of minutes later she came down the stairs. She had changed into a blue blouse, tight pants, and black boots the came half way up her calf.

"Damn, kitten. You look gorgeous," he commented.

"Thank you," she spoke softly. "Ready to go?"

"Yeah, I'm all finished. I'll get started on it tomorrow," he assured her and took her hand in his.

Hand in hand they left the bakery. She locked up behind them and they walked across the street to his truck. He opened the passenger side door for her and helped her in. He kissed her cheek before closing the door and rushed around to the driver side.

"What level are we going to? I know each of the levels are different," BJ spoke when he got in the truck.

"Bryan said they'll be on level fifteen. It's like a theatre of sorts with live performances from what I hear." He started the truck. "Everybody should be there by now."

"Hmm, I've never been to that level. I've only been to the restaurant on level eighteen."

"Then it will be the first time for both of us. I don't normally go out. I usually just work and home."

"That's about like me, work and relax."

It didn't take long for them to get to Heads N' Tails since it was only nine blocks away from the bakery. After parking in the parking garage, he opened the passenger door for her. They held hands as they walked inside. Dare signed them in with Tyra at the lobby's front desk then went to the elevator. Bryan had assured him Tyra would add level fifteen to his membership card.

"Tell me more about your cabin," BJ said as the elevator door closed. "What do you do to relax?"

"Other than spend time with my feisty kitten?" He pulled her close and pressed his lips against hers. "I'm a simple man. My cabin is a small two bedroom. I like playing my guitar by a campfire or relaxing in the hot tub. There's a small lake not far from the cabin. It's a nice fishing spot."

"I love fishing. It's the thrill of the fight I get a kick out of." She smiled up at him.

"You're my kind of woman, kitten." He kissed the tip of her nose.

They arrived on level fifteen and the elevator dinged before the doors opened. At the end of a short hall, double doors opened into the theatre cub. It's fancier than Dare had expected. Though it didn't surprise him. Bryan and Tony put a lot of thought into each level.

They weaved through the tables looking for Bryan and the group. Dare spotted Tony with a tray of drinks and pointed him out to BJ. They turned in that direction and followed Tony to the group.

"You made it," Annette squealed when she noticed BJ.

"Well, Dare said you two would be here. I couldn't resist." BJ gave Annette a hug. "Dare, I want you to meet Braelynn and her husband Ronan. You already know Annette, Bryan, and Tony. So, I won't bother with introductions."

Dare shook their hands and pulled a chair out for BJ. He excused himself to fetch them some drinks since everyone already had theirs. He could have waited on the waitress, but the room was packed, so it would probably take a while. He ordered BJ a Fuzzy Navel and a draft beer for himself. He grabbed the drinks off the bar and headed back to the table. He set the Fuzzy Navel in front of BJ. She took a quick sniff before taking a sip.

"How did you know?" She took a second sip.

"I remember everything you tell me. You said it was your favorite. You've had a rough day and deserve your favorite drink," he replied and kissed her cheek.

"She needs vodka after almost turning into an ice cube," Annette stated. "Next time Sandra comes around get a round of shots for everyone."

"I'll go get a round." Bryan stood up.

"Thanks." Annette gave Bryan a kiss then he leaned over and kissed Tony before getting up from the table.

"I wouldn't have turned into an ice cube. I was in the cooler, remember?" BJ took another sip of her drink.

"Your lips were blue." Annette glared at BJ.

"How long were you in there?" Dare asked and put his arm around her shoulder.

"Only about an hour." BJ shrugged. "Thankfully it wasn't the freezer or I would have been in trouble."

"I wonder if that's the reason for trapping you in there," Dare suggested. "If you were gone, someone would be able to buy the property."

"I was thinking the same thing earlier. I'll be glad when the cameras are installed. That way, next time, I'll have all the proof the cops need to charge that asshole."

"I can't believe someone would do that just to get their hands on some property," Annette commented.

"You would be amazed at the length people will go for things they want," Ronan told Annette. "BJ, were you thinking about selling?"

"No, and especially not to him. I don't like the type that think they can get what they want by throwing their money in people's faces. I can't be bought," BJ told Ronan.

"Take precautions. They don't take no for an answer very well," Ronan warned.

"I was just telling Dare earlier that I'm having a security system with cameras installed." She looked over to Annette. "I called them after you left today. Their tech was out or it would have been today. I'll have to wait until Monday."

"Good, I'm glad you're taking this seriously." Annette pushed her drink aside as Bryan passed shots around the table. "Now the fun can begin."

For three hours, they talked and drank. He was actually having a good time with everyone. He didn't go out in crowds often. Tonight, he was more focused on BJ and the group rather than what was going on around him. He could tell the day had weighed heavily on BJ. Her small hand squeezed his thigh as his arm wrapped around her shoulders, pulling her a little closer. He lightly kissed her cheek and asked if she was ready to leave. Her slight nod was all he needed.

"Bryan, you mind if I show BJ what we're working on?" he asked. It would be the perfect excuse to leave.

"Yeah, go ahead. You did most of the work," Bryan gave the okay.

"We're going to head on down there before we leave. Thanks for the invite, it was a pleasure." He stood and pulled BJ chair out for her.

They said their goodbyes. BJ went around the table, giving Annette and Braelynn hugs. He took her hand when she came back to him and lead her to the main door. BJ didn't speak on the ride down, instead she laid her head against his chest.

"Would you rather head straight out?" he asked, worried she was exhausted.

"No, I want to see where you go every day," she said sweetly.

"You sure? You look tired," he commented.

"Yeah, what type of club is on the twelfth level?" She righted herself.

"I'm not sure what type, I just know the design. It's one of my favorites," he admitted.

"Why is that?"

"You'll see? It caters to those that are closer to nature," he said as the elevator dinged and the door slid open.

He took her through the double door that led into the club. It wasn't finished, but the bar and some of the columns were finished. The tables had come in early and were spread throughout the club. He held her hand and led her to the bar.

"You did that?" She pointed to the detailed carving on the bar.

"Yep, down to every last leaf." He ran his hand along the front of the bar.

The forest scene had taken him weeks to complete. Ivy and small flowers weaved through the trees. Animals were hidden throughout the forest. The columns held the same detail on a larger scale. BJ ran her hand along one of the finished columns.

"These really are amazing. You can pretty much carve anything, huh?" she asked, and he nodded. "So, you can carve a tiger on my half door?"

"Anything for you." He pressed his lips against hers.

"I want a tiger." She held back a yawn.

"You already got me, but I think I need to get you home," he offered. "I was going to see if you wanted to come back to my cabin. You know, come check out where I spend my nights without you."

"I really want to see your cabin, but I think I'll have to take a raincheck." She finally let her yawn out. He tried hard to fight the yawn that threatened to escape. It came out anyway, causing BJ to laugh.

"Come on, kitten. Let's get you home." He put his arm around her as they headed out.

On the way back to the Bakery, BJ had fallen asleep. He parked right in front of the bakery so she wouldn't have to walk that far. He woke her up and took her keys. She was drowsy, so it was easier for him to unlock the door. He checked her apartment before leaving her to lock up behind him. He waited out front until she cut off the lights and went upstairs to her apartment. He pulled away when the lights came on upstairs.

Eleven

The bakery continued to have a slow showing of customers. More rumors were no doubt spreading around thanks to Mr. Jones and whoever he had working for him. BJ hoped it would pass soon. The rumors would die out and become a thing of the past and she would still be here. At least she still had some big orders from restaurants. It would have to be her bread and butter until her normal customers came back. *Annette should be here shorty to pick up Tobias' order.* She thought about the order and remembered she had to call Annette. Her cell phone was upstairs on charge so she used the landline. When she put the phone up to her ear, a lot of static crackled in her ear. She hung the phone up and picked it back up, hoping the static was a glitch. Static was still in the line. She called Annette's number but no one answered. BJ hung the phone back on the base as the bell over the door chimed.

"I was just trying to call you," she told Annette when she walked through the door.

"Business slow again?" Annette asked looking around as she came up to the counter.

"Oh no, a massive herd of people just left. Damn near wiped me out," she said sarcastically.

"Alright, smartass." Annette rolled her eyes. "What were you calling me for?"

"Oh, you didn't specify if Tobias wanted a topping on the cheesecake he added to the order." She didn't want to leave it bare if he wanted a topping.

"Shit, I left my phone at home." Annette checked all her pockets. "Can I use yours?"

"Mine's on charge," she answered. "You can use the landline. It's a little staticky. It's been like that since yesterday. I keep hoping I'll pick it up and it's magically fixed itself."

BJ wiped down the counter while Annette tried to talk to Tobias over the static.

"No, he wants it plain." Annette hung up the phone. "He needs a list of pies you make. He mentioned something about bears liking pies," Annette laughed.

"I can make practically any type of pie he wants." She pulled out a menu she had been working on. Each item had been listed and priced for singles or batches. "It's just a rough copy, but he can look over these."

"Excellent." Annette took the paper menu.

BJ went into the freezer to get the trays of yeast rolls Tobias ordered. She stacked the covered trays and brought them out to the sales counter.

"Wow, that's a stack." Annette's eyes widened.

"Hold on, I think I may have a box in the back we can put these in. Might make it a little easier to carry." Annette followed her to the back.

"You and Dare have plans tonight?" Annette asked holding the storage room door open.

"I haven't call him. I didn't realize in my buzzed state that when I plugged my charger into my phone that I accidentally unplugged my charger from the wall. I went half the day not even knowing my phone was dead."

"Bummer." Annette frowned. "I can pass a message to him on my way up to the restaurant."

"No, it will be okay. I think he has the day off today." She stacked the trays into the box she found then placed the cheesecake on top. "You need some help carrying this out?"

"You can get the door for me. I parked right in front." Annette scooped up the box and headed for the door.

After Annette left, BJ called the telephone company. After telling them the problem, they agreed to come out by closing time today to take a look. An hour later a technician in a white jumper came through the door.

"You got here quicker than I expected," she said when he introduced himself.

"I was in the area on another call when dispatch called."

"Well the sooner the better," she said. "It's right this way."

She showed him where the phone was and let him have his space to work. She watched as he worked and fumbled around with the phone base.

"What's that?" she asked as he slid something from the bottom of the phone base.

"Oh, nothing." He slid it into his bag.

"I saw you pull something from the phone."

"That? It was a magnet to catch any loose components in the phone." He placed the phone back on the counter. He listened to the phone and put it back on the hook and repeated the process.

BJ didn't believe him, but didn't think he had a reason to lie to her either. He handed her the phone. The static was gone. The technician left just as quickly as he came. Normally, she would've had to sign something showing he was there. If he needed her signature, he'd be back. She shrugged it off. She had other things to do than worry about his paperwork.

For the first time in months, BJ decided not to bake anything else that day. She didn't want to waste food or time. She could spend the last few hours of work reading a book. She ran up stairs and grabbed her romance novel from the end table in her living room. On her way back down stairs, the bell chimed out. She rushed down the last few steps. A technician came in wearing a blue work jumper. He introduced himself as being from the same company.

"Needed my signature after all?" She knew he forgot something.

"I do but after I fix the phone. Which one is it?" he asked stepping up to the counter.

"A technician named Dylan already fixed it. I thought you came back to get my signature."

"No one works with us by that name," he told her. He looked at his phone and turned it toward her. "See? The work order is still active. Who ever fixed your phone wasn't with us."

"Then who was he?" she asked.

"Was he wearing a suit like this?" He waved his hand down his side. "Or a badge like this?" He held up his work idea badge that was hanging from his left pocket.

"No, his jumper was white and he didn't have a badge."

"Then he wasn't with this company," he told her.

"Do you use magnets?" she asked on a whim.

"No, for what?"

"The man pulled something off the bottom of my phone he said it was a magnet he used but I don't remember him grabbing it from his bag."

"Maybe it was a bug," he suggested. "They're not that hard to come by. There are different sizes but most I've seen are about the size of a round magnet. Fits in the palm of your hand, easy to conceal. Just stick it to a surface and you can hear everything going on in the room."

"Well, fudge nugget, that's not good."

"Your husband suspects something," the young man said.

"Excuse you?"

"Most times when someone has been bugged like that is because their spouse suspects them of cheating," he told her with a shrug. "It's not my place to judge."

"I assure you that's not the case." But she did know someone who might gain from it.

"Well, if your phone is fixed, I'll be heading out to the next work order. If you'll just sign here indicating you no longer needed servicing." He handed her his phone and stylus to sign her name.

"Thanks for coming out. You were helpful regardless," she said as he walked out.

How could Mr. Jones have gotten the device under her phone without her knowing. If he did it the night of the rat incident then she would have heard the static for the past few days. The first time she remembered the static was yesterday when she called for the security system to be put in. He did it while she was stuck in the cooler. He must have been the person that came in before Annette. Nothing was missing because they came in to plant the bug. She searched high and low for anything out of the ordinary. She couldn't call the cops with no proof that anything was even there to begin with.

By 6 o'clock she had only served a couple of customers. She was ready to lock up for the evening. She still needed to search her apartment in case Mr. Jones was able to get any devices up there. She locked the bakery door and pushed to make sure it was indeed locked. On her way up to her apartment she turned off all the lights in the bakery.

She looked around in her apartment, checking under everything that moved. She felt creeped out by the thought of someone listening in on her every moment. She turned on the radio and turned the volume up. If anyone was listening in, they were going to have a headache. She turned it up another notch for good measure. Tonight, she was going to relax and finish that book. She went to her kitchen to preheat the oven then pulled a small chicken pot pie out of the freezer. It would take almost an hour to cook, so she'd have plenty of time to jump in the shower.

Waiting for the oven to preheat, she went to the bedroom. She grabbed her panties from the dresser.

The stove beeped as she walked into the bathroom. Placing her panties by the sink, she went to the kitchen. She stuck the chicken pot pie in the oven and set the timer. On the way back to bathroom one of her favorite songs came on the radio. Her body swayed with the music. Singing along with Shania Twain, she stripped her clothes off, throwing them into the dirty clothes hamper. She turned the hot water on with just a little bit of cold. Steam rose up to the ceiling. Stepping into the shower the hot water jetted down onto her body. It was the pounding of the water on her back that had her choosing a shower over a hot bath.

The only thing that would have been better at that moment was if she was at Dare's cabin with him in the hot tub. Last night she wanted to go to his cabin, but she could barely hold her eyes open. She wouldn't have been any fun. Plus, she would rather see his place when she could actual remember it. Maybe he'd play his guitar for her and even sing a little. She washed up with thoughts of Dare in the shower with her. His touch was gentle the other night and exactly what she needed. Everyone was right, she needed to let go of Dave and move on, and Dare was the perfect one to do it with.

The music suddenly cut off. *What the hell?* Quietly, she listened for another song to start as she rinsed the shampoo from her hair. When the music didn't start back, she turned off the shower and pulled the curtain open. Surrounded by steam, she stepped out of the shower and wrapped her towel around herself. She heard a crackling and she pulled open the bathroom door. Her apartment was in flames. The fire crackled as flames licked away at her window curtains. All her exits were blocked included a way out of the bathroom. Realizing the severity of her situation she screamed to the top of her lungs.

Twelve

Dare wasn't able to sleep when he got home from dropping BJ off last night. Instead, he grabbed a beer and started working on her half door. He worked through the night and all morning, but he managed to finish it a day early. Finally tired, he managed to grab a few hours of sleep in the afternoon.

He slept longer than he wanted to. Looking at his phone, there were no missed calls. He left her alone to do her thing today, hoping she would find clarity to their relationship. He checked his phone again when he got out of the shower. Not hearing from BJ didn't sit well with him, but he did promise to give her some space.

Coming up with a plan, he decided to use the half door as an excuse to pop in. He just needed to know that she was okay, without coming off as being worried or possessive. Carefully, he loaded the wrapped half door into the bed of his truck. The look on her face would be worth it when she saw what he carved. Getting in the driver seat, he started the truck. Leaving behind his quiet cabin by the woods, he headed into the city. It was a longer drive than it would have been from Heads N' Tails. By the time he got there, BJ would have closed the bakery. Thinking he should grab some food on the way, he tossed the idea. Maybe she had already eaten or she may want to go out to eat.

As he was approaching, the bakery the door opened. It wasn't BJ slinking out of the door. The lights were off. She had already closed for the night. Pressing the gas, he sped up. Slamming on the breaks, he pulled to a stop in front of the bakery. He opened his door and jumped out. *This asshole wasn't getting away this time.* Dare took off in a run. The man ran down the alley beside the bakery. Dare was faster though. Letting his tiger free, he shifted. He never missed a beat. When he was behind the man, he pounced, bringing all his tiger weight down on the unsuspecting man. Without using his claws, he swatted the man to flip him over. The young man screamed in a high-pitched voice. It wasn't Mr. Jones like he expected. Dare shifted back but left his tiger paw on the young man's chest.

"What did you do in there?" he demanded.

"Please don't kill me," the man cried.

A crackling sound caught Dare's attention. He looked up toward the window of BJ's apartment where flames were rising.

"Son of a bitch! If she dies, you die." He slammed the man's head down, knocking him out.

Jumping up, he slung the man over his shoulders. He ran into the bakery with the man bouncing against his back. Stashing him in the cooler, Dare trapped him in. Once he got BJ out, he'd come back for the man. BJ's scream echoed through the building. Taking the steps three at a time, he ran upstairs. The door to her apartment was already on fire and smoke was filling the upstairs ceiling. Kicking through the flames, his foot hit the door. It broke from the hinges and landed a few feet from the entrance. BJ was standing at the bathroom door, swatting at the flames with a towel. She must have been in the shower. All she was wearing was a towel

"Dare!" Her scream pierced through his heart. *Not again.* He wasn't going to let the fire take BJ too.

"Take some towels into the shower and turn the cold water on. I'm coming to get you," he yelled to her.

She disappeared into the bathroom. The flames grew and the crackling got louder. Stepping back into the hallway, he shifted into his tiger. He ran in and jumped over the fire blocking the doorway. He dodged the burning table. The smoke on the ceiling began to get lower as more smoke formed. He leapt over the flames and into the bathroom. He shifted the second he landed. BJ was standing under the water in the shower. He ran over to her and gave her a quick hug.

"I don't know what happened," she spoke as he picked up the wet towels from the bottom of the tub.

"Someone started the fire." He draped wet towels around her so the flames wouldn't get her skin. He draped another over her head. "It will protect you from the smoke. When I shift, climb on to my back and hold on for your life."

"What about you?" she asked with a terror in her eyes.

"I'll be alright. I'll heal quicker than you. We're wasting too much time." The moment the words left his mouth, she pressed her lips against his.

She took a step back and he shifted in front of her. Facing the door, he backed up for her to get on. He jerked when a cold towel was draped over him rather than her climbing on.

"You need to be safe too." She climbed onto his back, tucking her feet underneath him. "I'm ready."

Her arms went around his neck. He was going to get her out of this. The flames completed their way around the door frame, creating a ring of fire. Wishing he had more running space, he backed up as far as he could until his hind legs hit the side of the tub. The creak of a board breaking had him shooting forward. He leapt through the doorway, his fur singeing from the flames. He roared out and BJ squeezed on tighter. Without stopping, he dodged the flames. A beam cracked in the ceiling over the couch. Flames trapped them in at the door. He leapt through the flames, knowing BJ would be safe under the wet towels. The flames touched his stomach, burning his fur and skin. He didn't have time to react. He ran down the steps.

"I'm slipping," she said sliding forward.

Almost there. Holding his head up he kept her from falling as they made it down the rest of the way. Sirens rang out in the distance. Another loud crack sounded as they reached the bakery kitchen. Frantic pounding and yelling came from inside the cooler. BJ jumped from his back, dropping some towels as she ran to a stool and grabbed her cardigan.

Keeping true to his word, Dare shifted and opened the cooler. The man tried to run past him but Dare wasn't letting him go anywhere. He grabbed him by his throat, bringing him to a dead stop. BJ ran outside while he escorted their fire starter out.

"When the cops get here, you will tell them everything," Dare ordered him.

"I have nothing to say," the man hissed out.

Dare slammed him down on the table by the door. Partially shifting his hand, he borrowed his tiger's claws to instill fear. The man's eyes widened and panic began to creep in. Dare fished around in the man's pockets until he found his wallet. Looking at the man's driver's license and photos, he smiled.

"Well now, Dylan Miller. You will tell them everything, or I'll come for you." Dare slipped a family photo into his back pocket. He scraped his claw down the man's throat. "You wouldn't believe what a lonely tiger like me is capable of. I do love a good game of cat and mouse." His claw nicked the man's skin and a bead of blood formed. "I trust you'll do the right thing."

Dylan nodded and Dare let him up but didn't let him go. They walked out as the firefighters were pulling up at a safe distance. BJ was tucked away in his truck, safe from people's prying eye. He crossed the street with his prisoner. When BJ caught sight of them, she jumped out of the truck.

"You're the man pretending to be from the telephone company." BJ pointed her finger at the man as they walked up to the truck. Her knee came up, connecting with Dylan's manhood. He went down on his knees and Dare let go. BJ balled up her fist and punched him in the nose. "That's for my bakery."

The commotion got the attention of the officer on scene. Dare handed Dylan over to the police. The officer on scene was the same one from the night of the rat incident. The officer cuffed Dylan and detained him until he got all the statements he needed. Dare pulled Dylan's family photo out of his pocket and showed it to BJ.

"Hey, that's the woman that locked me in the cooler, yesterday." BJ took the photo from him. She told the officer what happened and about the bug Dylan must have planted in her phone.

"We'll get everything sorted out." He shook their hands. "I'm glad you were able to make it out."

"I wouldn't have if it wasn't for Dare." BJ looked up at him.

"You did a fine job." He clapped Dare on the back and walked back to his police car.

"How did you know I was in trouble?" BJ asked him.

"I didn't. I came over to bring you the half door I finished today." He nodded to the back of his truck.

"Looks like I don't need it right now." Frowning, she looked back to her bakery.

What didn't burn was getting plenty of water damage. He couldn't imagine what she was going through at this moment. That bakery was her everything.

"Will you come back to my place? Stay a few days until you figure things out," he offered. "I have an extra bedroom. I promise I will still give you your space."

"I don't need anymore space." She wrapped her arms around his neck. "You'll be there and that's all I need."

"After Sarah died, I didn't think I'd love again." He kissed her lips. "You've won my heart already, kitten."

"Take me back to your cabin." She kissed him. She didn't have to tell him twice.

"After you, kitten." He opened the truck door for her to slide inside. She slid over to the passenger side and he slid in next to her. "Let's go home."

Thirteen

"Wow, this place is beautiful." They pulled up in front of his log cabin.

"It's simple." He shrugged. "Come on, I'll show you around."

She got out of the passenger side and adjusted her cardigan. His simple cabin had a wrap around porch. A large workshop sat to the right of the cabin. They went inside, and he showed her the layout. It was simple but beautiful. Each piece of furniture was handcrafted by Dare. He took her out to the back porch. It was bigger than the front porch and had a patio attached. There was a hot tub in the corner of the porch. A larger grill and smoker were on the patio a few yards from the hot tub. With the floodlights on, she could see a fire pit in the middle of the back yard.

Right now, she didn't even want to look at a fire. Standing against the porch railing, she stared at the fire pit. Ashes and burnt wood were in the center from previous fires. The fire at her apartment flashed before her eyes. Flames lit up her living room. Heat from the flames dampened her skin with beads of sweat. Smoke rolled up to the ceiling, finally escaping when the window busted. Her kitchen was even ablaze by the time they got out.

"I think I burned my dinner." She tried to smile but it wasn't happening. Her stomach growled, protesting to the lack of food.

"I have some steaks in the refrigerator. How about I grill them while you rest your body in the hot tub? I saw you eyeballing it." He uncovered the hot tub, placing the big cover behind it.

"Water is good." She walked over to him and wrapped her arms around his neck. "Why don't you hop in too?"

"I have a little healing to do before I get in the water. Maybe after dinner." He placed a kiss on her forehead and pressed the button for the jets.

"Healing?" Stepping back, she looked him over. "You don't look hurt."

"It's not bad." He unbuttoned his shirt exposing his stomach. "It just doesn't look pretty at the moment."

"Why are your clothes not burned?" His skinned was charred in patches, but his clothes were untouched.

"Because I wasn't wearing clothes as a tiger. I don't understand all the magic in shifting. Some shifter's clothes shred to pieces, others can shift with their clothes still intact. I happen to be one of those. I'll heal fast, give it an hour or two and there will barely be a scar. Tomorrow, you won't even know I was burned."

"Wow, that fast?" Smiling, she pulled his shirt the rest of the way off.

"Shifter perks." He leaned down and captured her lips with his. "I should start the grill."

He went down the steps and over to the grill. While he started the grill, he kept glancing up at her. With a grin, she dropped her cardigan to the porch floor. His eyes were locked on her body. She slowly climbed into the hot tub.

"Damn, kitten." He shook his head as he came back up the steps.

"What?" She watched as he walked over to her.

"Gorgeous." He bent over the hot tub and kissed her lips. "I'm going to get the steaks ready."

As he stood, she glanced down at his stomach. She could tell the healing process had already started. His skin no longer looked charred, but rather had deep angry red marks with a few black specks. Resting back onto the headrest, she let the jets massage her back.

She wouldn't be here if it wasn't for Dare. He had risked his life to save her. Not everyone would run into a burning building, most would call the fire department and leave it for them. Instead, he ran inside not knowing how bad it was going to be. Dare didn't have to say it for her to know that he loved her. She could feel it in everything he did. She needed to live and be complete again. Dare could complete her.

Dare was so much like Dave was, yet different. He was much like Dave wanted to be. Everything that was hers and Dave's burned in the fire. It was time she let him go for good. He'd always be in her heart, but now was the time for her to focus on her happiness. Dare was who made her happy. She could easily spend forever with him.

"Deep thoughts?" Dare came out of the cabin with a plate of steaks and a towel. He dropped the towel on the chair by the hot tub.

"A few." She watched as he went down the steps. "I was wondering if any of my stuff survived the fire."

"I'll take you by there tomorrow, but we'll have to check the stability of the building before you can go in. I'm not letting you go up those stairs if the whole thing could collapse."

"I know," she sighed.

Dare's phone rang from his pocket. He answered the phone, but didn't stay on long.

Instead he came up the steps and held out his phone to her.

"For me?" She wiped her hands on the towel he had placed in the chair.

"It's the sheriff." He handed her the phone.

"Hello?" she spoke into the phone expecting more bad news.

"Ms. Elwood, sorry to disturb you so late. I wanted to let you know that Dylan Miller confessed to everything, including who hired him. We're picking up Mr. Jones now. It's over, with Mr. Miller's confession and testimony we'll have a case against Mr. Jones."

"That's great news. I'm surprised he confessed to attempted murder and arson." She looked up at Dare, who only shrugged and went back to the grill.

She watched Dare flip the steaks over as she listened to the sheriff. After a minute, she hung up the phone and dropped it on the towel.

"Dylan confessed to everything," she told Dare. "Said he would confess once the sheriff promised you wouldn't go anywhere near him or his family. You know anything about that?"

"I may have given him the impression that if he didn't tell the truth, bad things would happen." Shrugging, he pulled the steaks off the grill.

"Did you have to threaten him?" she asked as he walked up the porch steps.

"He told the truth, didn't he?"

"Yes, he did and they're going to pick up Mr. Jones, too." Grabbing the towel, she stood from the hot tub. "Steaks smell good."

"Dry off and have a seat." He motioned to the table and chairs on the other end of the porch. "I'll plate up dinner and bring it out."

Once she dried off, she wrapped the towel around her. Picking up her cardigan, she smelled the fabric. It reeked of smoke. She dropped it back to the porch floor. The back door opened and Dare came out with two plates and a shirt thrown over his shoulder. He placed the plates on the table and handed her the shirt.

"I thought you might like to cover up with more than a towel. Though I wouldn't mind if you didn't." He winked at her. "I'll grab us some drinks."

While he went inside for drinks, she slipped the shirt over her head and let the towel fall from around her. She picked it up and spread it out over the railing to dry. When she sat down, Dare came out with two glasses of sweet tea and set one next to her plate. Cutting into her steak, she took a bite.

"Oh, this is wonderful. How did you know I liked it medium rare?" she asked taking another bite.

"It's how you ordered it on our first date," he reminded her.

"That's right." She took another bite. "I think you could give Tobias a run for his money."

"Tobias?" he asked with a raised brow.

"He's the chef at the restaurant," she told him.

"Should I be jealous of his spices?" He smiled and took a bite of his rare steak.

"I love the way you spice your meat." She took another bite. "You cooked it to perfection."

"Wait until you taste my ribs. The meat will practically fall off the bone." He started on his salad.

"Ribs are another one of my favorites." She finished off her steak.

"We'll have to pick some up tomorrow on our way back from your place." He put down his fork. "I can help you rebuild if you want. I can make you an amazing display."

Thinking about his offer, she took a bite of her salad. The bakery wouldn't be the same after the fire. It wouldn't hold the same memories. Her home was destroyed.

"I'm not sure I want to rebuild. I have insurance on the place. It will cover the losses." It's not how she wanted to go out, but maybe it was a blessing in disguise.

"What will you do?"

"I want to buy a boat." She stood and picked up her plate. "Maybe I'll get my captain's license and take people fishing."

They took the dishes into the kitchen to wash them. Dare went out to clean the grill. Unsure of what to do with herself, she followed him out. Staring at his back, she watched him. His muscles were toned and she would love to have her hands on him. She imagined rubbing baby oil over his muscles. He turned around, and she was left looking at his healing stomach. All that was left of his burn was red puffy skin. It healed too fast to be real except she had seen it with her own eyes. She studied him as he came up the steps, stopping in front of her.

"Amazing." She reached her hand out and gently touched his raised skin. "Want to get in the hot tub now?"

"Absolutely." He took her hand and helped her up.

He bent down and kissed her forehead. His hands gathered the hem of her shirt. She raised her arms for him to take her shirt off. She stood completely bare for him to see. She wasn't nervous in the least. He wanted her, not a hot young model, just her. She could tell he only had eyes for her. His attention at the club was focused purely on her. She'd take the plunge that Braelynn and Annette told her about. She knew shifters mated for life. She could handle life with Dare.

It took her by surprise when he picked her up. She let out a playful squeal as he turned toward the hot tub. He set her in, then pushed his jeans down. Turning toward him, she backed up against the jet and watched as he bent over to take his jeans off. She could watch him forever. The way his muscles moved and flex with each task. Her body reacted to his. Her heart raced as he stepped into the hot tub and took the seat next to her. He laid his head back and she knew the jets were hitting him just right. His face mirrored hers earlier. She turned and came up between his legs. Placing kisses on his chest, flicking his nipple ring with her tongue. Her body pressed against his as the jets swirled the water around them. He wrapped his arms around her, and pulled her up to straddle him. Claiming his lips, she pressed her body against him. His hard mass rested between her ass cheeks.

"Be my kitten forever," he whispered to her.

"You want me as your mate?"

"I would run through the fiery pits of hell for you." She could see the truth in his eyes.

"I think the fiery pits of my apartment were enough." Smiling, she kissed his lips.

"Enough for you to say yes?"

"Yes," she laughed as he stood, taking her with him. She wrapped her legs around his waist. "Where are we going?"

"I want to claim you and make you mine." He stepped out of the hot tub. "As much as I love water sex, I'd rather lay you down in front of me."

He claimed her lips as he carried her through the cabin. Most of the lights were off but that didn't seem to phase him. Entering the bedroom, he reached out his arm and turned on the lights. Dimming the settings, he gave the room a romantic glow. Crossing the room, he laid her in the center of the bed.

He crawled on the bed, positioning himself between her legs. He massaged her calves and up her thighs. His hands felt wonderful against her body. Her legs had been aching for days with her being on her feet all the time. His hands traveled up her body, fingers lightly teasing her core. He would get close to her waiting, yearning opening, then pull away. He crushed his lips to hers as his thumb circled over her throbbing clit. The sensitivity made her body jerk. His lips curled up in a smile yet didn't leave her lips. She loved kissing this man. He trailed kisses down her body. He gathered her breast in his hand, taking her nipple into his mouth. He nibbled lightly, sending thrill chills down her body. She wrapped her hand in his hair, pulling him closer to her. He suckled on her nipple and flicked over it with his tongue. Her nipple a stiff mound, he moved to her other breast. His hard cock pressed against her slick opening.

Spreading her legs, she invited him in. He sat back and pushed the head of his cock into her tight opening. Grabbing her hips, he pulled her closer to him and down on his shaft. Slowly, he filled her with every inch of him. His thumb circled her clit in time with each thrust. His movements were slow as if he was trying to take his time. Each thrust brought her closer to her climax.

Unexpectedly, he pulled completely out. He climbed off the side of the bed. For a moment, she wondered what happened until she noticed his grin. He grabbed her ankles and pulled her to the side of the bed. Gently he flipped her over and she went willingly. He pulled her closer to the edge and buried his cock in her again. The sudden fullness had her moaning out loud. Reaching around her, he found her clit again. His thrust had more force, and she cried out in pleasure. He leaned down over her and took her breast in his hand. He pinched her nipple in time with his deep thrusts. She could feel him swelling inside her. Her muscles

Roxanne Witherell

tightened as her orgasm flowed through her. His body shuddered on top of her with his own release. He bit down on her shoulder and her orgasm hit again, this time gushing. Her eyes rolled to the back of her head, and she moaned out. His final thrust left her breathless. She never had an orgasm like that, never had she came so hard in her life.

"You're mine now, kitten." He kissed her shoulder where he had bitten as he pulled out of her.

"I like the sound of that." Her body rolled over and relaxed on the bed.

"I love you, BJ. I'll spend the rest of my life proving I can make you happy." He came down on top of her. He kissed her lips and trailed his lips down her neck.

"You already do." She looked him in the eyes. "I love you, Dare. I can't think of a better way to move forward than to move forward with you."

While she took a shower, Dare changed the wet sheets on the bed. It was the first night of

177

the rest of her life and she got to spend it in the arms of the man she loved. For such a terrible night, it ended up being one of the best nights of her life.

Epilogue

They ate dinner with Braelynn and Ronan at the Heads N' Tails' restaurant. Annette came over when her shift ended. Bryan and Tony joined them when coverage came in. Everyone was around the table again and BJ couldn't be happier. She lightly squeezed Dare's thigh and kissed his cheek.

"You two are too adorable together," Annette commented.

"Oh, tigers don't do adorable." BJ smiled over at Dare and patted his legs.

"Though she is right, we look good together." He pulled her chair closer to his.

"Congratulations, I knew you two would hit it off." Gerri stopped by the table.

"Congratulations for what?" Annette asked.

"The claiming, of course," Geri stated it like it was obvious.

"We were going to congratulate them, but we were waiting until they told everyone," Tony said looking between the two of them.

"How did you know already?" BJ asked Tony.

"Smell," Tony, Bryan and Ronan said in unison. She instinctively sniffed her arm to try and catch the smell.

"Damn, you could have told me I stink," BJ laughed.

"No, kitten." Dare patted her leg. "Once you've been claimed, your body has my scent. It tells other shifters that you're taken."

"As long as it's not a bad scent. I don't mind smelling like you." She shrugged.

"I assure you, it's not a bad thing," Gerri told her. "Have a wonderful time everyone."

"Where are you running off to? Don't you want to stay for a drink?" BJ offered.

"No, I must be getting down to the tenth level. There's a fox that needs a little reassurance," Gerri responded.

"Isn't that the strip club level?" Annette asked.

"Yep, dancers are some of the most difficult clients. It's proving difficult to find the perfect match for her," Gerri grimaced.

"I have faith in you," BJ told her. "After all, you accepted the challenge of finding Dare for me."

"It wasn't a challenge at all. The moment I saw him, I knew you two were meant to be." She glanced down at her watch. "I'll see everyone around I'm sure, but I really must be going."

Everyone said their farewells, and Gerri left the restaurant in search of her next client. Bryan ordered a round of celebratory shots. Annette and Braelynn both came around the table and gave BJ a hug.

"Are you just going to move in with him since your place is ruined?" Annette asked, taking her seat in between Tony and Bryan.

"Once the insurance pays out, I'm going to sell the property." BJ shrugged.

"Why? You loved the bakery," Annette asked. "Tobias said you could use the kitchen here to make rolls for the restaurant until you get your bakery back up and running."

"It won't be the same. I can still make rolls for the restaurant, but I'm not opening another bakery."

"You better not sell to McNeilsons. They're the reason all this happened in the first place," Annette commented.

"Oh, hell no! I meant it when I said they wouldn't be getting their slimy fingers on it. Someone else will come along who wants to buy it," BJ told her.

"What about me?" Ronan asked her. "I'll buy it from you whenever you're ready to sell it. I have shifters coming in all the time looking to settle in this area. I can promise you McNeilsons will never have it."

"You'll be the first one I call." And she meant it. Once everything was cleared, she'd sell it to Ronan.

After a couple of hours, BJ was ready to go back to the cabin. She was ready to have Dare all to herself. As if he could sense her readiness, Dare excused them from the party with tales of getting her to bed. BJ made her round of hugging her girls.

"I can't thank you two enough from blindsiding me with Gerri. I couldn't have picked a better man for myself."

"I told you she has the magical touch," Annette laughed.

"Have a great night!" Braelynn waved them off.

"Oh, I intend to." BJ slid her arm around Dare's.

"Let's go home," Dare said as the elevator door closed.

He wrapped her in his arms. His lips met hers in a passionate kiss. She melted into him as her knees weakened. She was going to enjoy this lifetime with her tiger.

"I may not have Bite My Bagel anymore, but at least I can still bite my Bengal." She nibbled on his neck and lightly kissed where she bit.

"Kitten, you can bite me anywhere as long as those sweet lips kiss it when you're done." He took possession of her lips, claiming them with his.

Bite my Bengal

This was how she wanted to spend the rest of her life. This was her forever.

ABOUT THE AUTHOR

Living in South Carolina Roxanne enjoys spending time with her family. Books are her escape from a house full of boys. When nerf wars are at a high, she can escape into her own little corner to create an escape for others.

Currently writing paranormal romance Roxanne has plans of dipping into other genres as well. Come and escape into the unknown.

www.facebook.com/AuthorRoxanneWitherell
www.twitter.com/RoxanneAuthor

More books by Roxanne Witherell

O'Neil Pack Series

Mountainside Resort

Fated Temptation

Missing Mate

Remember Mate

Paranormal Dating Agency

Winged Solution

For the Love of Fire and Ice

Paranormal Dating Agency World

Thank you for reading my contribution to the PDA World!

Reviews are greatly appreciated.

For more amazing stories in the PDA World follow us on Social Media:

MT World Press website:

http://mtworldspress.com/

MT Shared Worlds Reader Group:

https://www.facebook.com/groups/41296916
2428913/

MT Worlds Facebook page:

https://www.facebook.com/AlphaPNR/

email: mtwpress1@gmail.com

Made in the USA
Columbia, SC
03 March 2019